JESS BOWERS

HORSE SHOW

25 YEARS *sf*WP)

sfwp.com

Library of Congress Cataloging-in-Publication Data
Names: Bowers, Jess, 1980- author.
Title: Horse show / Jess Bowers.
Description: Santa Fe, NM : SFWP, [2024] | Summary: "From the tale of Lady,
   the mare who read a Duke University psychologist's mind, to television
   palomino Mr. Ed's hypnotic hold over Wilbur Post, the thirteen tales in
   Horse Show explore how humans have used, abused, and spectacularized
   their equine companions throughout American history. Wrestling with
   themes of obsolescence, grief, and nostalgia, Bowers guides us through
   her museum of equine esoterica with arresting imagery, unflinching
   intensity, and dark humor"—Provided by publisher.
Identifiers: LCCN 2023016842 (print) | LCCN 2023016843 (ebook) |
   ISBN 9781951631314 (trade paperback) | ISBN 9781951631321 (ebook)
Subjects: LCGFT: Short stories.
Classification: LCC PS3602.O8964 H67 2024 (print) | LCC PS3602.O8964
   (ebook) | DDC 813/.6—dc23/eng/20230602
LC record available at https://lccn.loc.gov/2023016842
LC ebook record available at https://lccn.loc.gov/2023016843

Published by SFWP
369 Montezuma Ave. #350
Santa Fe, NM 87501
sfwp.com

For Billy, who carried me

TABLE OF CONTENTS

THE MAMMOTH HORSE WAITS

The Wonder of The Age!

THE LARGEST HORSE IN THE WORLD!

Now Exhibiting At

Egyptian Hall, Piccadilly,

THE MAMMOTH HORSE,

General Washington,

The Property of Mr. Carter, the Lion King.

He is Twenty Hands in height, weighs
Twenty-five Hundred Pounds, and is the most remarkable Animal,
as regards size and shape, that was ever seen.

He will be exhibited from 12 till 4 o'clock each day.

ADMISSION — ONE SHILLING

**Mr. C. Will Give £1000 for a
MATCH to the MAMMOTH HORSE!**

Ladies and gentlemen, boys and girls, I must admit that it didn't surprise me in the least to discover that my friend Mr. Carter was still billing himself as the Lion King as late as 1846. Of course, he'd sworn he was done with that life years before, citing the high cost of beefsteak, the dozens of charlatans operating imitation big cat shows in London, and his latest grievous bodily injury, which had very nearly gone septic. Nonetheless, Carter maintained a sizable menagerie of man-eating lions in Brighton, so I'd long assumed he'd recover his wilder self soon enough. But from the moment I arrived at his London rooms that November, my friend was raving about something he called "a more genteel brand of rational family amusement," something sounding distinctly at odds with his former savage glory.

I remember looking forward to steering him off the topic over some pints. You see, my brief return to England was not purely a social call. At that time, I was attempting to establish a circus back in Connecticut, and I'd found it impossible to buy the exotic livestock I required from local suppliers. Carter had lions and jaguars to spare. I'd come hoping to strike a bargain. Repeatedly, I tried to bring my old friend around to the subject, but he just kept on ranting about his latest acquisition, the centerpiece of his new plan to provide "educational, wholesome entertainment" to the masses—the world's first and only "mammoth horse."

Carter called the beast "General Washington." Initially, he told me that he'd won it in a game of draughts, but that was before he'd arrived at a more satisfying explanation: that the noble steed was found galloping among a herd of mustangs on the Great Plains, and the combined might of twelve British-made steam engines was required to break his ironclad American will. This was the patriotic myth he trotted out for an informal gathering of fellow expatriate showmen in the back room of the Lamb and Flag, in a brazen attempt to outshine Phineas Taylor Barnum, king of us all, who presided over our private table with a benevolent eye. Barnum was in London at the behest of Queen Victoria herself, and his celebrated little person, General Tom Thumb, was the toast of the town. The great showman seemed to possess endless reserves of mirth and Cuban cigars. He passed both around our table like a favorite uncle dispensing sweets.

"That's marvelous, just marvelous," he crowed, puffing on his third cigar. "The Mammoth Horse! Reminds me of the 'Woolly Horse' I have back in New York, sole survivor of a native species now believed to be completely extinct, common ancestor to the deer, camel, buffalo, and giraffe. My European scout found it pulling a fruit cart in Austria—can you imagine? I now exhibit the beast alongside a blonde Circassian beauty who spins its wool into souvenir yarn. Very popular with the housewives."

For our brotherhood of Yankee showmen, the entertainments presented at London's Egyptian Hall marked the Copernican center of the universe. A visit from Barnum, our rising star, was a rare occasion to be drawn into his orbit, to bask in the reflected glow of his growing wealth and fame. And then there was Carter, his chapped lips drawn tight beneath his scrupulously waxed mustache. It was no secret that Barnum and Thumb's triumphant arrival had knocked the Lion King off his precarious throne. People were looking at Barnum, not Carter, and that was more than my proud friend could ever abide.

"Both beasts eat hay, and that's where the similarities end," he snapped. "I assure you there's no wool or glue involved in my act. Yes, Barnum, I've seen your 'Woolly Horse.' It is—like some others I might name—little more than an ass in sheep's clothing."

"Oh, well done, Carter!" bellowed Barnum, oblivious, or perhaps too polite. "I do enjoy being 'found out.' You see, in the end, I find that no matter what's being said about my exhibits, the public's craving to 'see it for themselves' tends to triumph. Why, just last month, a woman swore that the whale who dwells in the basement of my American Museum was molded out of India rubber, made to float and sink with hydraulic lifts! But she paid to see it just the same. Carter, I'm sure your 'big horse' is as big as the next man's, and if it's not, well, they'll pay to see the lifts nailed to its feet, won't they?"

"It's bigger than yours," slurred Carter. It was a bad joke, a drunk's joke, but several among us howled like schoolboys, slapping our palms on the sticky table. I myself was not immune.

"Well, perhaps I'll look in on it," said Barnum. "I have an appointment at the Hall tomorrow to see about securing rooms there. It's high time that *my* General, the celebrated Thumb, was introduced to her Majesty's subjects."

This was big news. The mere *rumor* of Barnum's miniature man at the Egyptian Hall would turn that modest showplace into a magnet for the rich and elite. But a full-scale Barnum production at the Hall, with the impresario himself presiding—*that* would make the rest of the exhibitors look like wet-eared amateurs. In short, the dwarf could dwarf us all.

I studied Carter carefully as Barnum described Tom Thumb's act, which involved a miniature trapeze, seven costume changes, and a dog. If there was one thing that my friend loathed in those days, it was being upstaged. Of course, it had been happening with some frequency since he'd quit the lion business, but somehow he still wasn't accustomed to it. And so, it wasn't long before Carter was theatrically clearing his throat.

"I wonder if you'd lend me your dwarf for a show or two," he interrupted. "Picture it—your tiny man upon the world's largest horse! The poster alone would draw in thousands. Everything fifty-fifty, of course. For the benefit of Barnum and Carter!"

Barnum chuckled indulgently, giving Carter a chance to fob the whole thing off as a joke. "I'm afraid I must decline on behalf of the

General's mother," he said. "I've signed affidavits ensuring that I'll bring her son safely back to Bridgeport."

Regrettably, one of the Lion King's more salient traits has always been his tendency, when roused by drink, to drive a moneymaking scheme to ground like a terrier hunting a vole. Carter's hand trotted drunkenly across the table toward Barnum's empty glass.

"Just picture it—Tom Thumb riding in, dressed as Napoleon!"

"He will do no such thing, sir."

"We'll make him do handstands on the horse's back!"

I was not eager to involve myself, but Barnum's nose was reddening, and he was reaching for his coat. I had to intercede on Carter's behalf, lest he set up a steeplechase course using the peppermill, or worse, draw the bush knife he habitually wore under his waistcoat. It used to be part of his costume, a mere prop, but lately he'd been brandishing it at inappropriate times. I reached over Carter's shoulder and pushed his galloping hand flat against the table, digging my fingernails into his knuckles.

Shock is an excellent way to gain an audience's attention. Carter stared up at me like a caught rabbit. There are moments in life when one must be very careful to say the right thing. So I mustered all of the social currency I held, and announced my intent to attend the mammoth horse's grand debut. It was, I reminded everyone, our professional duty as American showmen abroad to support one another's endeavors, despite the distasteful reality that, in the end, we all compete for the same awestruck gaze, the same sudden gasp, the same pocket money, so dearly earned, so credulously offered. Yes, I think I said something along those lines.

"Rufus Welch to the rescue! The generous Welch, who's got a heart like an ox, and is never happy unless he can see all happy around him!" shouted Barnum, clapping his hand on my shoulder. I had no idea I stood in such esteem. "I'll tag along," he said, "if only to verify that our Mr. Carter isn't putting one over on the trusting British public."

"Right, you mustn't be beaten at your own game," said Carter. But Barnum, always a gentleman, merely said his good days and left us all at the mercy of my drunken friend, who proceeded to present a free discourse on the prodigious quantities of hay that *his* General consumed each week. It was the death of the party. I did my best to bundle him home, with the help of a charitable coachman who, for two sovereigns, didn't mind cleaning the contents of my friend's stomach off his carriage floor.

I prefer to recall my friend as he once was, not as I found him that November in London. It seems necessary here to mention my own theory regarding Carter's famous bouts of dissipation, lest you assume that I voluntarily associate with charlatans and drunkards. For the better part of his adulthood, Mr. Carter, The American Lion King, took the stage thrice daily at the Egyptian Hall. Clad only in a striped bathing costume, he cracked his whip as heaps of snarling cats hurled themselves bodily at his naked chest. We have seen him drawn about the Egyptian Hall in a gilded cart lashed to a brace of Bengal tigers. We have seen him on the open stage of a theatre, taking a lion and lioness for a couch, two leopards for a counterpane, and a fearsome lynx for his pillow. Countless parlor walls are still papered with engravings of Mr. Carter rampant in watercolor jungles, using snakes as javelins, eternally hurling them toward a panther's red and waiting jaws. An artist, he was.

With luck, this is how history will choose to remember the man.

It is not how I found him when I arrived at Piccadilly the following afternoon. The London rain made the Egyptian Hall's "warm, dry interior" a surer draw than the savage allure of Catlin's "living Ojibbeway Indian tribe," though the shouting street boys made it clear that both attractions were cheaply available within.

In those days, before we traded imagination for the flickering delights of the nickelodeon, there were still true aficionados of the extraordinary. The crowds of worthies who swelled through our great Hall's vaulted doors shook out their wet umbrellas beside a herd of large stuffed exotics—including a giraffe, an elephant, and a Nubian lion—all tastefully arranged amid waxen models of tropical flora to create an instructive and curiously cozy illustration of a more torrid clime. The elephant was a special favorite of the children, posed as though it was still reaching for their peanuts and popcorn, its trunk reinforced with wire. I used to watch the boys and girls flock to it like small waterfowl, their governesses struggling them out of soggy cloaks so they could rub the beast's varnished snout for luck.

I was disappointed to learn that Carter was renting a small gallery at the back of the building, instead of the grand hall he'd commanded during his lion days. But he still drew a mob. The Cockney barker stationed in front of his new theatre still solemnly preached about the joys and wonders the Lion King offered within. Only now he touted General Washington, the Largest Horse in The World, here on a limited engagement from America, able to lift twice his weight in any substance, but gentle as a lamb! He bows and kneels on command! Next performance in just a few moments, right this way, sir and madam, right this way…

The snub-nosed youth tending the till covered the slot on Carter's coin-box when he saw me, and indicated a gap in the curtain behind him, beyond the reach of the jostling crowd. Thus instructed, I pummeled my way through dusty sailcloths, the air redolent of glue and lamp oil. Emerging from the swell of fabric, I found myself lost among the jungle of wires and pulleys and abandoned props that waits behind every stage—that bizarre paradise where dust bunnies gather wayward sequins and stagehands lurk, taking too much snuff.

Here, the mammoth horse waited among artificial ferns and the golden shambles of dismantled automata. His broad back was draped in the same burgundy bunting he wore in the advertisements. His hooves, the size of dinner plates, gleamed wet with bootblack. He was eating his hay, awaiting his cue.

The General's groom, a ruddy-cheeked lad, sat smoking, his pipe too large for his hand. You may know the type—he looked like he was born creeping under fences to gallop farmers' carthorses, living on dry oats and chaff, sleeping in straw under broodmares, blindly trusting that they wouldn't trample his ribs.

"*There's* Welch!" crowed Barnum, pounding his ivory-capped cane on the floor, startling both horse and boy. "I was beginning to worry. Coffee? Carter brought coffee. Awful stuff, but the horse makes up for it. A magnificent animal, isn't it, Welch? Nearly twenty-two hands at the shoulder, I'd say. No lifts on his feet—I've checked. Good teeth, too. But I can't say that this is the ideal venue. The fashionable set doesn't come here anymore, and there's no room to do the dangerous stunts that attract the working classes. Perhaps jumping through fiery hoops, under the big top, ridden bareback and bitless by an acrobatic woman? The beast could be trained."

I ventured to ask Barnum if he was reconsidering Carter's proposal.

"No, merely acknowledging the business potential. Of course, I won't make an offer until I've seen what it can do, other than stand there and be enormous."

The mammoth horse did this one thing exceedingly well, blinking his mulish eyes at us as he amiably chewed. Barnum suspected tranquilizers. For my part, I don't know what I'd expected, but it certainly wasn't this. I'd imagined flashing hooves and frothing mouth, perhaps—some modern Pegasus straining against his fetters. A large part of me longed for the sublime sense of danger found backstage at Carter's lion productions—the rancid stench of raw meat and dung, the sour clang of the big cats flinging their bulk against cage bars, threatening to break loose at any moment. But the wild Carterian jungle I remembered was long gone. His mammoth horse was inert and harmless, a bloated pumpkin at a county fair.

I was on the point of sharing these sad impressions with Barnum when the brassy bleat of a cornet turned our attention to the crowd beyond the curtain. The matinee show had drawn the usual rabble. Dandies, young couples in lust, nannies and their noisy charges—

all jockeyed for position at the lip of the stage. Their upturned faces looked buttered in the gaslight. A thousand eyes glittered expectantly. Taking the stage, Carter greeted his public with outstretched arms, his mellifluous voice ringing the room.

"Ladies and gentlemen, prepare to be astounded by a creature unlike any other! You are about to gaze upon the equine behemoth that I, Mr. Henry Carter, the American Lion King, captured galloping across my nation's great Western prairie! Ladies and gentlemen, the beast you are about to behold is a Titan among his species! Weighing in at twenty-five hundred pounds! Able to pull twice his weight from a dead standstill!"

The crowd absorbed this sermon with parted lips—the men toying anxiously with their hats, the ladies' perfumed bosoms heaving in delicate anticipation. All hung there, teetering at the brink of ecstasy, until the delicious moment when Carter, his broad chest lifted to the heavens, finally, luxuriously bellowed: MY FRIENDS, I GIVE YOU GENERAL WASHINGTON, THE LARGEST HORSE IN THE WORLD!

Now, I have seen this act many times before, in one form or another. After all, there are only so many ways that an unusually large animal can be exhibited in a public forum. But Carter's big horse was particularly excellent—easily the best of his kind. He followed his pet boy obediently, illustrating that he was, indeed, "gentle as a lamb." He stood stoically while his master extolled his beefy virtues, enduring comparisons to Alexander the Great's Bucephalus and a steam engine with equal aplomb. When the horse soiled the floor, an ingenious drainage system built specially for the purpose carried the offending fluid away before the ladies could pinch their noses. These marvels lulled us into a state of blithe amusement. We weren't ready.

"Now, it appears that neither man nor beast has appeared to challenge the might of Mr. Carter's Mammoth Horse!" said Carter, making a big show of scanning the crowd. "Some of you may not be aware of my standing offer of a thousand quid to anyone who can present a match to my Mammoth Horse in strength, size, and coloration. However, in the absence of any competition, the General shall hoist a two-ton mass of solid iron, generously forged for us by Mr. Nathaniel Bentley of Leadenhall Street, the first choice for all your ironmongery needs!"

On cue, an enormous, gilded weight gracefully descended from the rafters via an arcane web of pulleys and wires. It slowly ground to a halt at stage left, where the boy was already fitting a thick leather collar around the mammoth horse's bullish neck.

"Now, if I may have two volunteers from the audience to step up and assure themselves, with their own hands, that this weight is absolutely genuine...you, sir! And you there, madam, step right up..."

We watched as Carter led the young couple through a vaudevillian series of calisthenics and futile attempts to shift the weight. He asked them to repeat their exertions several times, though the mammoth horse seemed restive throughout, butting his enormous muzzle against the boy's cupped hands.

"No sense of timing," clucked Barnum, as the couple was finally allowed to descend, their cheeks red and puffy from their moment under the lights. At Carter's nod, the boy expertly hooked the horse's harness traces to the glinting weight. Then, with a flick of the whip, the real show began.

There was time to gape as the mammoth horse braced his broad chin against elephantine chest, his black haunches straining. There was time to gasp as the golden weight slowly, tremulously began to rise from the earthly confines of the stage floor. Our bodies vibrated marvelously in tune with the creaking floorboards. And for a moment, in the heaving presence of that equine dynamo, we were willing to believe that we were wrong. Surely the locomotive would never take the place of a good, sturdy carthorse. We were too rash in our decision to sell the children's cream pony, too quick to consign dear Old Jack's meat to the hounds, too eager to throw our lion king to the wolves. Yes, ladies and gentlemen—for a moment, we were well and truly *amazed.*

In the next, the mammoth horse sank, straining, to its knees. At first, there was every indication that this was a planned part of the act, the boy anxiously circling the beast's head, Carter confidently cracking his whip, the weight tantalizingly swaying an inch above the stage. We clapped. Then came the eerie creak of failing wood, and it was as though the floor grew a great wooden maw and swallowed the mammoth horse down into itself, pig-eyed and thrashing. His enormous hooves plunged for purchase against the splintering planks, his mouth a pink tangle of tongue and teeth. And then he went down for good and all, disappearing in a gray plume of dust and plaster, whinnying for a herd that never came.

***

Ladies and gentlemen, I wish I could say that we evacuated the theatre cleanly and efficiently, with minimum panic. I want to refer you to the fascinating eyewitness account of the porter's wife, who was the startled recipient of the mammoth horse's hind end as he descended into her basement apartment, smashing her grandfather clock "to atoms" with his flailing hooves. I want to tell you that her velveteen divan safely broke his fall, though his fall broke the divan. I want to say that the momentary aura of danger and violence generated by General Washington's death-defying stunt suffused Carter's flagging career with a new vitality, and how Carter, in gratitude, sent the mammoth horse to live out his natural allotment of days feasting on corn and clover, his broken body bathed and mended by a Circassian beauty. I want to say that death was, indeed, defied. I want to say that Carter and I kept in touch after he violently refused to sell me any of his precious lions, that we remained the best of friends, that he didn't drink himself to death in a London pool hall, pouring every red cent he had down his gullet.

In short, I find myself compelled to lie to you—and I suppose that, in the end, makes General Rufus Welch little better than Barnum or Carter.

In fact, the mammoth horse's sudden descent through the floor didn't kill it. After the veterinarian Carter summoned declared that the beast would never pull again, he said it was useless and got his rifle, right there in the porter's drawing room. I believe the meat went to his lions. Picture him roughly slinging the steaks through the iron bars, a brown bottle clenched between his teeth. The obituaries said he'd been considering reviving his old act. But his widow wrote me shortly thereafter, making it clear that she'd gilded the lily a bit in some regards, to preserve what little family dignity remained. She was auctioning off Carter's personal effects through one of the big houses in London and asked if there was anything of his that I particularly wanted.

The beast's skeleton arrived on my doorstep in an enormous wooden crate, two weeks after Mrs. Carter's letter. I had it mounted just as you see it. It resided in my study for many years before I decided that we both deserved another chance to tread the boards.

Perhaps you feel cheated to learn that the glossy black stallion painted on the sign outside is yet another exaggeration—that all that awaited you was an equine skeleton rubbed smooth by fingerprints and borax, clumsily articulated with excelsior and wire. Alas, the mammoth horse's mortal remains can only provide the meanest hint of its enormous size, and I, with my imperfect memory, cannot do justice to the creature's short and inimitable career. You've paid your nickel, and if what there is to see here doesn't meet your expectations, I am more than happy to refund it.

But please, before that unpleasant business, indulge an old showman one last time. Take a moment to picture the noble crest of the neck, the scent of horseflesh and gaslight, the gentle nicker of happier times. Run your fingers along his enormous brow. Trace the hollow pits that held his liquid eyes. And try to remember that little golden age between the horse and the automobile, when we still had wonder.

Then, and only then, may you ask for your money back.

TWO ON
A HORSE

Number One

The black horse on the inside rail is the fastest. The beach urchins know these quick physics, wrestle each other through the turnstiles to claim him, calling dibs. For luck, they rub the bald spot where his paint's worn thin, then jerk their burnt fingers away from the sunbaked metal. He takes many names—Thunder, Jack, Man O' War—but "Number One" is what the carnies shout when he wins, plucking stuffed ponies and doll-babies from pegboards, pressing them into sticky ice cream hands.

To break the dark horse's centrifugal spell, you must first bribe fat Hetty O'Brien with promises of red hots and half-used ride tickets, dredged out of trashcans where yellowjackets swarm for soda and sting. If there are fewer than twenty-five holes pockmarking your ticket's toothy cartoon face, you can wipe off the mustard and ride anything, free of charge. The Steeplechase is the main attraction. "Half a Mile in Half a Minute - And Fun all the way!"

Fat Hetty hates the horses, but she loves free rides on the Trip to the Moon. When she's not holding court under the boardwalk, you will find her in that dim cyclorama, gazing starry-eyed at the pictures that fly past as the room spins on steel rollers. The running joke is that she craves the mid-show snack of moldy cheese, scraped from the lunar surface by costumed Selenites. Really, she goes to dream of joining their glimmering ranks. Someday, she will take her rightful place among them, and leap out in sea-green silk and sequins, feet festooned with jingling sleigh bells, the first girl on the moon.

Hetty O'Brien smells of boiled cigarettes and cabbage, but you pinch your nose and endure, because her weight will send any horse plunging into first as soon as the bugle sounds—wheels giddily whizzing down the metal rails, wind stinging your wet teeth. The signs say "hold fast," but that won't stop you from waving at the landlubbers below. They say "don't look down," but that's just a double-dare.

And for a holy moment you are soaring, the ocean a distant gray whale.

Number Three

The gray has long been the ladies' favorite, good old lucky number three. He was called "the white" in the early days, back when he was factory fresh and unicorn-new, but that first coat of paint rubbed off long ago. Now hard gray wads of forgotten gum cling between his legs, and some of his wooden mane has been chunked away with penknives. But Victorias and Bessies alike still choose him, wheedling their dates and brothers away from the black horse or the brown with wide, entreating eyes.

Debutantes, housewives, match girls—all were expected to ride sidesaddle, legs swept uselessly to the left, petticoats billowing. These elegant handicaps made the gray horse the safest bet, since only his wheels are welded securely into the center of the elevated track, well away from the sheer drops on either side, where a caught hem or gust of salted air can get you smashed like popcorn on the pavement below. Everyone knows someone who knew someone who saw it happen—a woman sidesaddle on number four slid to the wooden floor under the track, where she got smacked bloody by her friends' horses. A thousand shoes flung from dangling toes. Babes-in-arms dropped between the rails, tiny scalps dented like Kewpie dolls. The ride had no brakes.

These were but a few of the horrors that the suffragist Eugenia Clare evoked during her modestly publicized lecture at rival Dreamland Park, situated cattycorner to Steeplechase's caparisoned spires.

Though she herself was not an avid horseback rider, the diminutive Miss Eugenia claimed that sitting aside on a Steeplechase mannequin was far more dangerous than doing so on a well-trained animal. A real horse is a slave to human reason, not gravity, she cried. What's more, some bright spark had the Steeplechase ponies jointed at the shoulder, so that layers of metal would flex realistically as each horse circled the Pavilion of Fun. After one painful experience, gentlemen learned to beware worn saddles and stand up in the irons when going over a whoop-dee-doo. But where did that leave the unfortunate woman who, hobbled by modesty, could not rise?

Miss Eugenia concluded her sermon by declaring that she herself intended to ride Steeplechase astride, and what's more, any woman wishing to view her demonstration would receive admission to that park free of charge. Dreamland authorities attempted to block her from leaving the lecture hall, but that only drew a larger crowd. She was a lightning rod in a rust-colored split skirt, her whip swinging at her uncorseted waist. The papers said that she stormed the gates at Steeplechase Park in the company of at least thirty clamorous reformers. It must have been a quiet war. The owner, George Tilyou, was expecting her, had sent a retinue of attendants dressed in jockey silks to escort her up the five-story spiral staircase that led to the park's signature ride. Rubberneckers cluttered the pavement below the racetrack, hoping for a glimpse of revolution or lacy bloomers.

The signs in the mounting area said two to a horse, but it had been arranged in advance that Miss Eugenia should ride alone. Of course she was given first choice. She had honestly thought that she'd like to ride a horse-rollercoaster, the way she used to love merry-go-rounds. That's what she'd imagined when she agreed to this stunt, sight unseen: a pony fantasia, pastel rumps festooned with gold, or flowers, or *fleur de lis*, each carved steed a different child's dream. Tilyou's five horses come molded to match and match and match, frozen in mid-stride, awful in their symmetry. Seeing them, she spooked, her heart a moth behind her ribs.

The crowd began to murmur that she wouldn't go through with it. The lady-reformers slated to ride alongside her questioned first her nerve, then their own. But before anyone could speak, Miss Eugenia Clare took a sharp bolt of salt air and strode toward the white horse, swinging aboard before Tilyou himself could offer a leg-up.

Those who watched Miss Eugenia swoop through the sky at Steeplechase naturally assumed that she, like so many women before her, chose the white for safety alone. But really they were all compelled by some deep-boned half-memory—a childhood pony ride, the soap-sweet scent of Mother clutching them against a brass carousel pole, or a storybook engraving of the lady-centaur Godiva, become her own white knight.

Number Two, Number Four

There have always been two brown horses on the Coney Island Steeplechase. This was originally a concession to realism—the ride's German manufacturer, like everyone else in those days, had simply seen enough horseflesh to know that it usually comes in brown. But long after the last New York streetcar unhitched its equine engine, it remained tradition to keep two browns on the ride. Along with the black, they make their odd-colored stablemates stand out, shiny gray and bay against the robin's egg sky.

Now the flappers and sheiks come down to the sea in Fords, hot leather backseats sticky under the bathing-suit knees of girls with Clara Bow mouths and rough names like Charlie or Dot. They are a package deal, like most tenement sheilas. If a fella wants to show Charlie a good time, Dot's got to come too, for deep is the dread of the boardwalk belly dancers' shimmy-shake, of Charlie's arms flung about Harry's neck, or Dot's creamy Irish thighs cushioning a stranger's sudden tumble on the Flopper—instant moral ruin. Each girl is meant to preserve the other's virtue, in a jungle of machines subtly engineered to press skin against skin. It is well known among the swinging youth of America that the right cocktail of gravity and terror will turn the demurest girl into a wild-eyed clutcher—and so they swarm the turnstiles at Steeplechase, combination tickets (Harry's treat!) safe in hand, pink threads of spun sugar stuck to sun-chapped lips.

Charlie and Dot end up on the browns, they are just the type: too busy fussing over who's riding with whom to care which horse they take, too fizzy from the gin picnic Harry passed around behind the Loop-de-Loops, he's so thoughtful to have brought a flask. Of course he clambers up behind Charlie on horse number four, they've been on the make all day. Poor Dot is left to the tender mercies of a sallow fellow in a straw boater, some vague acquaintance she's been trying to shake since the Human Pool Table, where he careened into her headfirst. He says his name is Pete, but she'd swear he originally introduced himself as Paul, and this (plus gin) makes her nervous. She dilly-dallys behind horse number two as long as she can, hoping he'll get on first. But he's crouching beside the horse's shoulder, interlocked palms outstretched, and the old bugler looks ready to get this show on the road, so she must mount.

The brown horse's springs shudder as he swings up behind her, his sweaty heft pressed close against her back. Dot can smell the gum in his mouth, sour mint and dentistry. She thinks she should've worn the blue skirt. It would've covered her legs more.

And they're off—greased wheels clattering in steel housings as the horses gain momentum, rattling the wooden supports until the whole boneshaking works feels like it's creaking toward imminent collapse. Of course Harry's football weight sends Charlie zooming ahead, whooping and laughing and look-ma-no-handsing as they rattle around the near turn. The horses on either side blur as they blow by, transforming into bright smears of bathing suits and gleaming metal. The wind roars past Dot's ears, drowns out the calliope. At the first turn, the sallow man leans hard into her, one clammy hand fumbling with her breasts, the other creeping up her thigh.

She screams, but everyone is screaming. Halfway down, she shuts her eyes.

Number Five

The blood bay on the far rail is always the last horse chosen, and with good reason. His orbit swings out a full six feet farther than the number four mannequin, perilously close to the gingerbread-thin rail that separates the track from open sky. Though the finest views of the beach beyond are available from the bay's back, he is reserved for the daredevils and thrillbillies, those foolish few who swallow their churning stomachs and place utter trust in inertia.

Pupetta Gargiulo is his secret queen, though you'd never know it to see her punching dough in her father's Surf Avenue pizzeria, flour dusting her black hair, butter smudging her puggy nose. The nickel slices at Gargiulo's are the biggest on the boardwalk, so the front window stays busy most weekends, when sandy customers throng the counter to watch Uncle Giuseppe spin the dough. From her station in the back of the shop, Pupi can just see the tops of their heads, sunburnt red as marinara. When thunderstorms blow in, the scent of grease and ozone sifts through the propped screen door, and customers collect under the awning for shelter, where Papa cajoles them into buying whole pies. These are passed steaming over the counter like giant communion wafers, mozzarella baked into crisp brown lace.

Pupi is thirteen, but she has to stand on a soapbox to refill the mixer, making little avalanches of flour and salt. She pulls tangled dough off the beaters and throws it back into the bowl to be reabsorbed. Dinner rush ends around sundown, then they sit on crates in the alley, listening to the sky pop as fireworks chase the workaday crowds back to Brooklyn. On good nights, Papa and Uncle Giuseppe smoke cheap cigarillos and divvy up the profits, one for him, one for him, a nickel for her. On bad nights, they drink.

Pupi's mother used to say that when the men are in the wine, it is best for women to be forgotten, kept out of sight. She used to shepherd Pupi down to the sea, her floury hands cupped around her daughter's shoulders, her swollen belly slicing through the crowd like a ship's prow. The doctor said it would have been a boy, a little Antonio or Carlo or Enzo, a strong young hook to hang the family's hopes upon.

His is the phantom hand in hers as she wanders up the strand, past beached jellyfish and forgotten sandwiches, damp from the sea. After the ocean gulps the last of the yolky sun, Coney is set ablaze. Shooting galleries and popcorn stands flash sodium bulbs. Most of the rides run late, advertising twice the thrills in the dark. At this hour, it's easy for a girl to limbo under the turnstiles, her petty crime camouflaged by drunken crowds clamoring for cut-price admission to the illuminated swimming pool. High above it all, the Steeplechase slices the sky like a comet, its metal skeleton limned in fairy light, the dark drop beneath the rails making the ride seem twice as high. The five wooden horses carry on careening down the artificial hill, with or without screeching jockeys. A winner is called, then they are pulleyed up backwards to await the next leg of their endless race. Pupi squirrels her shoes away behind the wooden box that conceals the mechanism and scales the sandy stairs barefoot. A year ago, she was scared to ride the Steeplechase horses. A year ago, she didn't have to melt into the bedroom wall and watch as Giuseppe reels onto her, reeking of anchovies and gin.

Now Pupi picks the bay every night, or he picks her. No one helps her climb onto his back, or tells her to wind the soft leather reins around her fingers. If the ride attendant looked up from the funny papers, he might be surprised to spot such a young girl alone in the saddle at this hour, her bare feet barely grazing the stirrups, her hair backlit by the orangeade sky. But still he pulls the lever that sends her horse soaring out into the black, lights flashing, heart churning, near heaven.

Nobody ever asks Pupetta Gargiulo where she lives. If they did, she would not mention her father's green-roofed pizzeria—instead, she would point to the long straightaway abutting the Pavilion of Fun, where the track is smoothest. When the bay's nose passes the quarter pole, she holds steady for a second, pressing her feet into the irons. Quick as a whip, she ducks under the reins, shimmying the leather down over her shoulders until it comes to rest around her waist. Then she braces herself atop the speeding machine, albatross arms outstretched, her smile a three-ring circus.

ONE TRICK PONY

DATE: 31st AUG, 1938
SCENE: 2B
TAKE: 12

Jesse James's getaway horse won't jump off a cliff, no matter how fast ace
stuntman Cliff Lyons gallops her, snorting, toward the yawning edge.

For four hours now the film crew has been working on this stunt,
destined to be the equestrian centerpiece of *Jesse James* (1939). They've
tried whips and spurs, hollering and waving, even threw lit firecrackers
at the little mare's hindlegs, hoping to panic her over. Now they have
her wearing movie blinkers: serene equine eyes painted on a dainty
headstall, invisible in an extreme long shot. Tricks just like these have
taught us horses in the Wild West loved to china-shop through saloons,
collapse over tripwires, and soar boldly off fifty-foot cliffs under heavy
gunfire—so utter was their devotion to the American cowboy.

But ace stuntman Cliff Lyons is careless on his first approach—he
doesn't gallop fast enough, giving his mount time to notice the land
is ending. All twelve subsequent jump attempts have ended with the
little mare skidding to a halt, crow-hopping and shaking her mane at
the abyss: a hard no.

On the shore below, Twentieth Century Fox contract director
Henry King's threadbare patience frays. He's spent six months preparing
to shoot five seconds, scouting the ideal ratio of sublime crag to rangy
poplar, consulting depth charts. Anachronistically poured in 1931,
decades after the James Gang rode the range, the manmade Lake of the
Ozarks remains the only deep-water lake in Missouri. It rests several
counties away from the production's home base in sleepy Pineville,

Missouri, where a star-struck city council let his crew bury Main Street under fill dirt and nail wooden facades over the storefronts downtown: Justice of the Peace, Acme Tool Company, First National Bank of Northfield. Due to these and other on-location expenses, Henry King's budget for *Jesse James* is already over a million dollars and climbing each second this goddamn horse doesn't jump off that goddamn cliff.

Seven cameras idle along the lakeshore like skeletal waterfowl, necks craned toward the lapping water, lenses black and waiting. Not for the first time, Henry King wishes he'd hired one of those diving girls he and his wife saw in Atlantic City to double Jesse instead. Some skullcapped waif in a red bathing suit would have already sailed that goddamn horse right off that goddamn cliff, easy as a paper airplane. Dress her like Jesse, tape down her gymnast chest, and no audience would spot the switcheroo—they'd be watching the horse, collective breath well and truly taken.

The epic shot Henry King imagines is somewhat out of character for a director barely footnoted today in accounts of classical Hollywood. To some degree, his lackluster reputation can be blamed on the saccharine dramadies Twentieth Century Fox gives him: soapy pap like *I Loved You Wednesday* (1933) and *Seventh Heaven* (1937). Less director than recorder of deeds, Henry King's "aesthetic" is a vague barrage of shot-reverse-shot, malingering close-ups, and medium long interiors. He frames shots like he's filming a play—a common error of directors who came up during the silent era nimbly avoided by the likes of Alfred Hitchcock and John Ford, King's more famous contemporaries. Even he can tell these men are destined to win at history, making him an also-ran. This is why he spends most nights drunk and alone on his terrace, the lit white letters of HOLLYWOODLAND gleaming like starlets' teeth from the black hills beyond.

A proud Virginian by birth, Henry King was intrigued by screenwriter Nunnally Johnson's barstool pitch to recast southerner Jesse James as a hero, not an outlaw. He liked the idea of the notorious

James brothers as just a couple of good, God-fearing guys driven to crime by the transcontinental railroad's unjust seizure of homesteaders' land—just the kind of heroes post-Depression America wanted. "About the only connection it had with fact," later said Jo Frances James, Jesse's elderly granddaughter, "was there was a man named James and he did ride a horse."

Fox Pictures heartthrob-in-the-making Tyrone Power would play Jesse. Brunette ingenue Nancy Kelly signed on as Jesse's estranged wife Zerelda, while up-and-comer Henry Fonda took the role of Frank James. Veteran character actor Ernest Whitman, whose filmography includes roles such as King Malaba in *Drums of the Congo* (1942), and Black Man Talking To Himself (uncredited) in *The Lost Weekend* (1945), portrayed Pinkie, the James boys' loyal Uncle Tom. Though Whitman gives a fine performance, the character is a clumsy attempt to whitewash the family's Confederate past. Whitman later reprised Pinkie alongside Henry Fonda in *The Return of Frank James* (1940), making him one of the first Black actors in Hollywood with a franchised speaking role, but this accomplishment is not what *Jesse James* (1939) gets remembered for, when it is remembered at all.

Studio head Darryl F. Zanuck greenlit the picture despite concern making Jesse James into a Depression-era Robin Hood would doom it everywhere but Missouri, where the infamous train robber already enjoyed folkloric status. Undeterred, Henry King insisted he shoot on-location in "real James Gang territory," an expensive 1,563 miles from Hollywood, claiming the verdant Ozark backcountry would set his new movie apart from the five other westerns being filmed simultaneously in the usual desolate corners of Nevada, New Mexico, and California.

Zanuck agreed. "It's hard to ruin a western," he said, signing the papers.

Now, on set, those words ring in Henry King's ears like a double dare. He slaps another mosquito dead, grinding its wiry body into the black hairs sprouting from a large mole on his right arm. He thinks about how Tyrone Power and Henry Fonda are being paid to nap in Airstream Clippers instead of playing Frank and Jesse James in Twentieth Century Fox's new western—the first ever shot in three color Technicolor. He squints at the lowering sun. By now he should be shooting Frank James scrambling onto the opposite shore under heavy but inaccurate gunfire. Or Jesse James treading water under a green tangle of ivy, left for dead by Frank, galloping off-screen as bullets rain the lake. Cut to Henry Fonda and Tyrone Power toweling off for the drive back to Pineville, the shot safely in the can.

"Goddamn horse is burning daylight!" King barks at no one in particular.

Among the poplars, assistant key grips scatter like startled quail.

DATE: 31st AUG, 1938
SCENE: 2B
TAKE: 14

The goddamn horse in question is named Babe, though this is known to no one on the crew of *Jesse James* save ace stuntman Cliff Lyons, who trained her himself as part of the stunt string he boards on Twentieth Century Fox's backlot, where Babe spends half her life.

The rest of the time she's surrounded by humans who wear too-clean clothes and shout at each other, her nose stuffed in a feedbag and her tail in a manure catcher until she's requested on set. Though uncredited, Babe has been background scenery in Roy Rogers' *Under Western Stars* (1938), marched in several studio parades, and performed a feature stunt in the Republic Pictures serial *Zorro Rides Again* (1937), where she leapt a five-foot wide gully without complaint, Cliff Lyons himself in the irons.

But today he's asking too much. As apex prey, every horse's brain is wired to protect the herd from hazards exactly like the cliff the humans keep trying to force Babe over. The fear of the first horse they tried hangs in her nostrils. When the herd says don't go, you don't— she learned this as a foal. Babe tries to convey this law with bucks and snorts and kicks, but this is semaphore ace stuntman Cliff Lyons can't or won't understand. When Henry King barks "action," Cliff claps his legs against Babe's sides and together they charge pell-mell down the trail leading to the jump-off. The little mare likes this part: the footing is soft for a gallop, and the trees streak by in an agreeable green blur. Down the stretch they come, horse's knees pumping, man's torso rigid, braced for flight. Then Babe skids to a halt thirty feet shy of the edge just like she said she would, flinging Cliff Lyons into a twisted, cussing heap.

When he sees the stunt still isn't happening, Henry King stalks uphill swinging his megaphone like a billy club. He is the unfortunate sort of person who cries when he's mad, and his eyes are swimming by the time he reaches a bloody Cliff Lyons. The cowboy dabs a scrape on his brow with his red bandana and explains how there's no sense in trying again today. Maybe not even tomorrow—the horses are too rattled. It'll take six hours round-trip to get another one from his stunt string. There's a buckskin gelding in Pineville yet who might do. But not till tomorrow: he won't haul his horses in the dark.

Henry King takes a deep draught of piney Ozark air and squeezes his eyes shut, sending tears down his sweaty cheeks. He believes in a version of himself who can calmly explain how he needs to see two horses leap like Pegasus, black hooves treading cloudless blue. He wants to (gently!) remind Cliff Lyons the trick he's failed at fourteen times is supposed to be the equestrian spectacle of this movie, the sequence to make cap gun-toting schoolboys *ooh* and *aah* and pester their friends to go see the new Jesse James picture again, two horses dive right off a cliff, it's swell!

Instead Henry King aims his megaphone at Cliff's square jaw and screams he is the worst goddamn stuntman in Hollywood, a sham and a cheat who needs to get back on that goddamn horse and do what he's being paid for, right goddamn now. Blinking, Cliff Lyons spits at the dirt, staring King down like he's just another ornery horse needing a come-to-Jesus moment.

Unlike Fox contract director Henry King, ace stuntman Cliff Lyons's career and reputation hangs on the movie he made last week, not last year. He is sunburnt and sore, with a hot shower and a cold beer waiting for him back in Pineville. This may help explain how and why Cliff Lyons, who history otherwise records as a thoughtful and humane horseman, ever agreed to what happened next.

DATE: 1st SEPT, 1938
SCENE: 2B
TAKE: 15

Invented by industrial agriculture to slide unwitting livestock into cloudy troughs of flea dip, the tilt chute is a steel platform enclosed on three sides by pipe railing, with a gate on one end to let animals in one at a time (cattle) or *en masse* (pigs, sheep, goats). The three-tiered railing prevents stock from escaping until the operator pulls a lever and the platform tilts, spilling the animal(s) into the drink. Once dunked, each bather scrabbles to its feet, shrugging off the chemicals, then trots up a corrugated ramp, making way for the next victim. Used correctly, the tilt chute is quick and humane.

It is also what Henry King and/or Cliff Lyons—blame is hazy— used to slide poor Babe into a dead drop seventy feet high. Greased with lard, a tilt chute is the reason why, in the final cut of *Jesse James*, Frank and Jesse's twin horses are not seen triumphantly soaring into open air, a trumpet fanfare heralding their graceful descent. Instead we see them falling, one horse after the other, in the same awful posture, silent and wrong.

The lead-up to the stunt looks spectacular: a posse thirty lawmen strong pursues Jesse and Frank at full gallop, soundtracked only by stampeding hooves and birds chirping. The James boys are faster; they develop a slight lead. Pulling up both horses, Frank James dismounts to make sure his brother's up for what's coming next. Jesse's been shot in the arm; he's in shock.

"We gotta keep going, son, hold on," slurs Henry Fonda, reaching up to shake a woozy Tyrone Power awake in the saddle, his leading man looks twisted in agony. "Now hold tight, Jesse, because there's only one way out of here! Are you holding on?"

Tyrone Power feebly nods, clinging to his saddle horn like a child. Quick cut to the lawmen gaining on them, their horses thundering around the bend the James boys just rode through as gunshots pepper the trees.

"Gee-yap!" hollers Henry Fonda, pretending to whip Tyrone Power's horse with a branch. As Power gallops off-screen, cut to Cliff Lyons galloping downhill on Babe until a strategically placed log forces her to jump.

Cut to a wide shot of the cliff: a quarried hulk of lined limestone dominates the right half of the movie screen. The way the camera is angled transforms the Lake of the Ozarks into a canyon river, obscuring the water beyond. Bushes on the blufftop rustle, and the stunt starts there, with Babe coaxed into a rear to make this look like a running jump. Then the tilt chute slides the mare's hooves out from under her and she drops. Crouched in the bushes beside the chute, Cliff Lyons jumps right after, windmilling black-jacketed arms to steer himself away from the horse as she backflops through empty blue space, forelegs tucked into fetal position, limp as a failed kite.

Cliff Lyons knew the plan ahead of time, so he is able to somersault into something resembling a dive before he hits water. Babe isn't so lucky. Her head jackknives backward as she smashes the surface; the splashdown enhanced in post-production by a foley artist punching a bucket somewhere in California.

The camera cuts to Cliff and Babe leaping over the log again, then a closer shot of the same stunt from a slightly different angle. This time Cliff's supposed to be Frank, not Jesse, and Babe is supposed to be Frank's horse. The fall is shown in grisly instant replay. Again we see the horse's spine chop the sky like a guillotine blade, visual déjà vu.

Afterward, the scene cuts to a bird's eye view of two wet horses paddling alongside a gasping Cliff Lyons-as-Frank James. But it's Henry Fonda-as-Frank who audiences see clamber ashore under heavy gunfire, then mount his horse to gallop off-screen, leaving his brother for dead.

Tyrone Power surfaces under a leafy canopy, concealed from the posse descending to the riverbank, his survival unsurprising.

Everyone knows Jesse James doesn't drown.

DATE: 1st SEPT, 1938
SCENE: 2B
TAKE: 16

Marketed by Twentieth Century Fox using taglines like "Motion Pictures' Supreme Epic!" "The Tremendous Dramatic Thrills of the Midwest's Lawless Era!" and "So Big and Sensational! Yet Capable of Stirring Your Tenderest Emotions!" Henry King's pet Western premiered in New York City on January 14th, 1939.

Early reviews were generous. *Variety* commended the movie's "consummate showmanship…pictorial magnificence…skillful and seasoned direction," and the "superlative performances" of its young cast, particularly Power and Fonda. *The New York Times* declared the film "the best screen entertainment of the year" and "an authentic American panorama, enriched by dialogue, characterization, and incidents imported directly from the Missouri hills."

Not one critic praised or damned or even mentioned the film's cliff dive set piece, which is odd, because the stunt is all *Jesse James* gets remembered for today, when it's remembered at all.

Of course, Henry King's cameras were still running when Babe resurfaced. Instinctively, she tried to right herself, legs thrashing at bad angles while ace stuntman Cliff Lyons swam ashore. Still in character, he didn't look back until he knew he was off-camera, since in the film's diegesis, Frank James would have cared far more about not being shot than what his horse was up to. When he did get a chance to look back at Babe, Cliff Lyons was surprised to find her dead, bobbing like a buoy in the middle of the lake. Some eyewitnesses swear they saw her back snap on impact, the water like a brick wall. Others insist she died of panic: too disoriented to know she should swim, she tried to run.

Either way, ace stuntman Cliff Lyons rowed out with the lifejacketed production assistants to dispose of the body the same way he'd dealt with drowned livestock during his ranch hand days. Babe's mane sculled like seaweed in the murky lake water. Cliff Lyons undid her soggy saddle and bridle, dragging them into the rowboat's bottom. Then he held the mare's stiff pasterns together so the PAs could tie on the rock he chose, a thick slab of gneiss leftover from when the lake was dug. It was quiet on the set as the little mare sank, her grave first marked by a column of bubbles, then by nothing at all.

A horse dying on set was the sort of accident a better director would have written out of their movie. A different man would have found another way to get the James boys off the cliff and into the next scene. But because he was stuck in the silent era, Henry King felt audiences wouldn't understand how both Frank and Jesse made it over the cliff without seeing the stunt twice. As he saw it, the only alternative to reusing the fatal footage was an unfinished movie.

In the cutting room, Henry King reviewed the cliff stunt enough times to develop a blind spot three seconds long. As a result, he was honestly shocked to learn how in one matinee after another, at the glorious zenith of his epic Technicolor Western, grown adults and children alike cover their faces or choke on their sodas, wide-eyed.

When confronted by the American Humane Association about the stunt, Twentieth Century Fox studio head Darryl F. Zanuck maintained though they did "lose" an animal during production, no horses die on screen in *Jesse James* (1939), which is true. Henry King's camera averts its guilty eye just after splashdown, like a father turning our heads away from something awful, fooling no one.

GRANDDAD
SWAM

We got a swimming pool one summer, like a television family.

There were eight of us out of diapers by the late 70s, eleven altogether, and each June our grandparents' farm became the family sleepaway camp, where we gave each other friction burns and sang rounds about poop. I was one of the middle boys, too small to pester Granddad about letting me drive the tractor, and too big to stay in the kitchen with Memaw, if it'd been any other summer.

But the heat wave brought us all sweating to the table, even Granddad, because Memaw hoarded the oscillating fans. She liked to watch *The Price Is Right* and *Let's Make A Deal* from the eye of her own tiny windstorm, where she chain-smoked and drank Diet Coke while our littlest cousins tumbled in hand-me-down playpens. The four steel fans surrounding the table rattled ominously, especially the big Lasko that lopped off my older brother Jim's left pointer fingertip one summer. He swore that if you looked close, you could still see the blood, dried brown on the spinning blade. *Get back*, Memaw barked whenever she caught us trying to switch it off and see.

We should have been outside, but outside was an oven. Adams County hadn't seen rain since May. The yard was bone dry, fractured with deep cracks that twisted our ankles when we tried to run. The sun got so hot we could feel ourselves crisping, and the parched air was like a giant mosquito, sucking water from skin.

Granddad never burnt—he baked, brown as a potato. At night the flickering blue light of the Zenith carved his features. We gathered around the T.V. on floor pillows, struggling through Lawrence Welk so we could beg to stay up for Carson. It all seemed so glamorous to us, even the bubbles—as if the bubbles blown in Hollywood were somehow shinier and longer lasting than the ones we made with Memaw's dish soap. Out there, they still had water to waste. Cameras luxuriously panned across overflowing swimming pools. *The Brady Bunch Variety Hour* even employed SCUBA cameramen to follow the leggy blue flutter of the show's *two* in-house synchronized swimming troupes, who performed their weekly water ballet in a special on-stage pool while Florence Henderson cooed "Love To Love You, Baby" under a hypnotically rotating disco ball.

It got to all of us after a while. But it got to Granddad most of all.

Our Granddad was the eldest son of a once-thriving Pennsylvania poultry dynasty. He and his siblings grew up in the hot dust of the henhouse, passing eggs over candles to spot the embryos glowing orange within. Pamphlets and advertisements from this period tout the meaty breasts of our family's famous hand-raised White Leghorns and Barred Rocks. Granddad was meant to take over the hatchery when he turned eighteen, so he ran the books all through high school. There are pictures of him poring over ledgers, inspecting incubators with a solemn, supervisory air. But he ended up going to Korea when his twin brother enlisted. By the time he returned (brotherless) to claim his feathery destiny, Perdue had bought out most of the local poultry concerns. The spring chick sale, which once attracted a mob of folks wanting to fill cardboard boxes with peeps, dwindled until it was just a handful of mothers wanting dyed chicks for their kids' Easter baskets.

After Perdue—he always intoned the word solemnly, like it was the name of a war—Granddad had to scale back the operation. He hatched just thirty dozen chicks one year, then ten dozen the next, until only a small flock remained for scrambled eggs and chicken dinners. The big henhouse became a small engine repair shop, and he started fixing vacuum cleaners and lawnmowers for the neighbors. Our grandparents had lived that way for as long as I could remember, whiling away their days with grandbabies and poorly oiled machines. But here's the thing. Granddad had been born in that big old farmhouse, but he wouldn't die there. The way things were going, he couldn't afford to, and he knew it. That's why the T.V. bothered him. He'd worked all his life, and all he ended up with was less than he'd started with; that and a box to beam his family images of a life none of them could afford.

So there we sat, sweating in front of reruns of *Gilligan's Island*. The millionaire and his wife were on, sipping cocktails out of coconut shells and pretending to want off this godforsaken island, and Granddad just got up and left. I remember thinking that he really had to *go*, since he didn't even wait for a commercial. But when the credits rolled, and he didn't return, I got curious. Granddad was out in the front yard, barely outlined by the weak light spilling from the house, tamping green tomato stakes into the hard ground, pacing out the distance between them. He didn't notice me until he'd finished, and even then, he didn't explain, only mussed my hair and muttered "never you mind," as if I'd been brave enough to ask what he was doing.

Before dawn, Granddad fired up the backhoe, which belched to life with a loud pop of diesel and soot, so loud it even woke the teenagers. Memaw ran out screaming something about azaleas, but it was too late—the machine's rusty teeth had already snapped them up, depositing the scraggly remains atop the dirt mound rising behind the corncrib. Granddad wielded the backhoe expertly, manipulating the levers that drove the machine's bucket into the earth, then coasting to a stop in front of his wife, who demanded an explanation.

News of the groundbreaking filtered down through us kids like sun tea in a jar. Soon the whole house was vibrating with anticipation. For days, we spent our afternoons crowded into the big bay window in the front room, jockeying for space among Memaw's dusty Hummels. The older boys made a game out of ducking behind the sofa whenever Granddad paused in his labor to glance at the house. We all feared his knack for spotting idle hands. No one wanted to end up like Jim and Kevin, who spent their summer afternoons hunched behind wheelbarrows of concrete mix, then sat sunburnt and sullen at the dinner table, wincing in red-shouldered pain as they passed the buttered peas.

It took a week for Granddad to finish construction, mainly because the deep end had to be trenched out by hand. He made Jim measure the corners three times. They had to be as perfectly square as the pools we knew from the Bradys' television vacations, each turquoise rectangle rimmed in toothpaste white, every glittering pool a jewel in a chain stretching from Adams County to Californ-i-a. He wanted his grandchildren to turn mermaid, our thin fingers waterlogged white. He longed to smell chlorine and zinc oxide on our skin when he tucked us in, that faintly chemical tang of America's elite.

Once he deemed the pit large enough, Granddad formed up the sides with plywood and covered them with Quikrete that crept across the bottom of the pool. This part of the process was fraught with argument. Granddad scolded Kevin for mixing it too thin. He snatched the wheelbarrow away from Jim, said he was doing it wrong. The rest of us stood silent, feeling really lucky we weren't involved, until the job was finished and Jim and Kevin got to carve their names in the cool cement edge of the shallow end, crowning their autographs with a big "Z" for Zorro. I was so jealous I could spit.

After the concrete set, Granddad anchored an aluminum ladder to the bottom with bricks that had fallen out of the barn foundation. Then someone turned on the hose. I don't remember why we never thought to smooth or sand anything first. I guess the heat pickled our brains. We all just stood watching the hose writhe against the sides, splashing the dry cement elephant gray. Memaw kept saying that we shouldn't get our hopes up, it wouldn't hold water, the yard was too thirsty. But once the concrete soaked through, a dusty liquid began to pool in the far corner, and she had to eat crow.

We all changed into our bathing suits hours before dinner. But the pool was only half-full by the time Memaw set out a dessert of stale Oreos, which we flung like Frisbees and rescued from the tall grass.

Granddad poured in half a jug of Clorox and said we could all get in early if we used the ladder. No horseplay, no funny business. Anyone who jumped or dove would be banished to the front room with no T.V. Of course Jim cannonballed. He still says that he would have spent a thousand nights alone with that dead screen just to be the first one in, the freshest egg.

That swimming pool cut our feet to shreds, but no one cared. We got in after breakfast and stayed in after dark, begging for just a few more minutes whenever Memaw turned off the porch light, scattering the moths. *Marco! Polo!* Our voices rang through the cedars. Jim and Kevin took turns playing lifeguard, but they were also the two who started the whirlpool when Memaw wasn't looking. They banked the corners like dolphins, soaking the grass, sweeping the rest of us along in a giggling tangle of sunburnt arms and inflatables. You had to kick strategically to avoid a scrape on the sides, and someone was always getting a noseful of water, or a strawberry, or a bruise from a green walnut, which we threw like tennis balls. Something just bad enough to cry about would happen, and Memaw would yell out the screen door that we had five seconds to knock it off, four, three, *two—*

Our grandparents never got in the pool, at least not with us. Memaw changed into a white bathing suit after her soaps, put the toddlers down for naps, and sunned in her plastic lawnchair, chain-smoking Kools. Granddad spent his afternoons doing small engine repair, or reseeding the dead grass in a futile battle against the drought. A rumor developed among us that he avoided the pool because he'd taken a fall through an icy stock pond. We mentally transposed his face onto little Harry Bailey in *It's A Wonderful Life* until we believed it was a documentary. That's why he wanted us to swim, insisted Jim: to arm us against undertow, and grant us the fins he never grew.

Only those whose weak bladders sent us fumbling for the toilet after midnight ever learned the truth. Granddad swam. You could see him through the bubbled glass of the upstairs bathroom window, standing barefoot at the water's edge, wielding a net made of Memaw's torn nylons. With a pair of bug-eyed goggles strapped around his balding head, he lifted out the dead beetles, combing the water clean. Next came calisthenics—some jerky sequence half-remembered from a Charles Atlas record, performed at 33 1/3 r.p.m. to spare his knees. He rolled his shoulders like a boxer, his elbows folded into mighty right angles. In these moments, there was a trace of the high school hero about him, the sinewy vigor of brass trophies and felted varsity letters. He stretched his arms toward the star-studded sky, laced his fingers (here's the church here's the steeple), and just as you thought *oh, he's going to di*—he dove, piercing the surface like a javelin.

Granddad swam slowly, turning his head to breathe. His legs churned just underwater, stirring up a small wake that followed him up and down the pool. Each stroke sent a hail of peeper frogs bounding into the grass. Drowsy chickens bit at half-drowned moths. And onward went Granddad, his farmer-tanned arms carving arcs in the mist rising off the water.

Soon July was stealing June. People started letting themselves say "drought" aloud, and there was widespread worry about putting enough hay up for the winter. But our swimming pool was always surrounded by a lush clover halo, so green it seemed spray-painted, a lone patch of golf course glory in a bunker of dust. Of course it attracted wildlife. First our dinner chickens ambled over to snap at crickets, their guts and gizzards mysteriously transforming wiry legs and antennae to white and dark meat. Then came the rabbit family who darted under the porch whenever we banged through the screen door. Drowned possums and raccoons were fished out with the skimmer, each tiny jaw a sawtoothed leer.

In retrospect, someone should have noted the slow increase in size, the gradual ascent through the animal kingdom. But none of us knew the neighbor man had horses until his gray mare wound up dead in our swimming pool.

Jim was the one to find her. Her white belly ballooned in the deep end, forcing the head and neck underwater, where the mane waved like gray seaweed. One rheumy eye stood open. Her teeth were buttered corn.

Granddad strode out of the house, snatched away the stick Jim was using to poke the body, and shooed the rest of us back from the water. Then he gritted his jaw and swore. Those of us who saw his midnight swims watched the math in his eyes—how long it had been since he went back to bed versus when the horse must have fallen into the pool. It was awful to picture the animal as it must have been—alone in the dark water, nostrils flaring, hooves slashing for purchase on the concrete until, exhausted, she gave herself up for drowned. Each of us privately agonized that we'd left the gate in the woods standing open, the one that separated Granddad's land from the neighbors' pasture, but nobody had the guts to go check if it was, lest we arouse suspicion. Instead we all wondered aloud how we hadn't heard a splash or a whinny in the night. Later Jim said that he *had* dreamt of horses galumphing down red cliffs, the Lone Ranger and Silver aiming six-guns at a lemonade sky.

Memaw already called the neighbor man. He came grinding down our access road in a big black Ford and a real cowboy hat. A half-grown hound leapt out of the flatbed before the truck came to a complete stop, then pointed at the horse corpse, nose and tail spellbound straight. *Well, that's no good,* said the neighbor man, cocking his finger at the mare as he stepped out of the cab. Job done, the hound shambled over to drink from the deep end, his tongue a pink ladle.

Jim laughed first—a high, pubescent bark that echoed off the barn. Then the neighbor man did too, and we all had permission, even Granddad, who was so grateful he accepted a cigarette even though he didn't smoke.

It's just one of those things, said the neighbor man, and then he explained how Miss Sugar couldn't see in the dark—moonblind, he called it. She probably just figured she'd waded into a stock pond. Maybe she thought there was still a shore to reach, a way to march up out of the water, shake it off and get back to eating that grass there. I tell you, he said, that's the greenest grass I've seen in months. No wonder she came over here, all we got left is last year's hay. Anyway, it's a shame about the pool. Seems like it was a nice setup for the kids.

He looked right at us then, and we older kids were suddenly conscious of our Hawaiian-print swimsuits, of the orange vinyl floaties clinging to the twins' chubby arms, all ridiculous next to the bloated, floating Miss Sugar.

Granddad made our communal apologies, touching the cigarette to his lips every now and then, but mostly just letting it burn. The dead horse bobbed slightly in the deep end. And maybe it was because September was just a few weeks away, or maybe he was fed up with Memaw's complaints about the water bill, but either way, Granddad and the neighbor man decided that they'd fill in the swimming pool instead of trying to haul the dead mare up out of the water.

Granddad piloted the backhoe, clods of grassy clay clinging to the machine's steel maw as it swung through the air. The neighbor man stood nearby, supervising. For the first fifteen loads of dirt, it didn't seem like much was happening. Rocks and silt swirled to the bottom of the swimming pool, making the horse bob like a foundered canoe. Eventually, the water thickened, sucking the mare's body down until only the point of her shoulder jutted out of the muck, dingy and white like old bone.

The neighbor man found the biggest rock he could, a monster slab of shale that had to be pried out from under the machine shed with crowbars. Jim and Kevin were drafted as additional pallbearers, and together the four men swung the rock out over the water, aiming for Miss Sugar's bare shoulder, which sank under the weight, burbling as it disappeared.

I remember we had one of the chickens for dinner, even though it wasn't Sunday. Granddad went out with his hatchet, and Memaw fired up the oven, and we all changed out of our swimsuits to watch *Hawaii*

5-0. I'm pretty sure the special food was meant as a consolation prize for losing the pool, but the kitchen got so hot sweat dripped onto our plates, and there was blood in the meat.

LADY, THE MIND-READING MARE

Hear now the legend of Lady Wonder: tell her nothing, she tells all.

There she was and is and always will be, cross-tied and magisterial in her box stall, watching Mrs. Claudia D. Fonda of Chesterfield, Virginia disappear into the tack room, where their equipment is locked nightly to deter teenage thieves and the wary neighbor women who sashay past the Fonda pew, crossing themselves against the evil eye.

First Mrs. Fonda wheels forth the sawed-off kinderklavier with its soldered-on doll's chair, cushioned throne of Pudgy the Pomeranian, canine virtuoso. Yapping, he weaves between Mrs. Fonda's legs as she wheels his instrument into the barn's sitting area. This lurid island of orange upholstery is where she knits when business gets slow, Pudgy snug in her lap.

Next comes the typewriter/xylophone. Handcrafted by Mr. Clarence Fonda, a miner for the Tredegar Iron Works, the contraption boasts thirty-six hinged tin keys, one for each letter of the alphabet, plus all ten digits, padded with sponge rubber. Portable, it clatters and squeaks across the barn floor on repurposed furniture casters. But the racket doesn't spook Lady Wonder, for whom the world's only typewriter/xylophone is as familiar and friendly as a halter and lead.

The horse snorts, expecting breakfast: two flakes of timothy hay is enough roughage to occupy her until noon, when they open up shop. But Mrs. Fonda doesn't feed her. Instead, she leaves to smoke a cigarette in front of the roadside sign she had Clarence repaint yesterday: LADY WONDER WILL SPELL AND SUBTRACT MULTIPLY DIVIDE TELLS TIME ANSWERS QUESTIONS. She frets about the white smudge he left under the Q.

Lady Wonder knows all, but that doesn't mean she can divine

why Mrs. Fonda reenters the barn reeking of tar and unease, then busies herself rearranging a vase of silk flowers. Lady Wonder whinnies disapproval, and receives a harsh shush. She can't tell that Mrs. Fonda is dressed for company, her ebony hair pinned with a rhinestone peacock, her patent-leather shoes buffed to a beetle shine. What Lady Wonder can sense is Mrs. Fonda's anxiety. She stretches her muzzle toward the padded keys. Working her lips around the lever, she flips the letter Y into place with a tinny click. Then she reaches for the worn E, and finally S—a familiar pattern that gets results.

This done, Lady Wonder butts her bony forehead against Mrs. Fonda's midsection, snuffling at her coat. But Mrs. Fonda does not praise her or draw a linty knuckle of carrot from her pocket. Instead she resets the letters, shaking her head.

***

What follows is a transcript of the business card enclosed in numerous letters sent unsolicited to Duke University's Psychology Department by the worried citizens of Chesterfield, Virginia.

PHONE   ADMISSION

82-0478   ADULT $1, CHILD 50¢

LADY WONDER

THE EDUCATED MIND READING HORSE

WILL ANSWER QUESTIONS

MRS. C.D. FONDA

PETERSBURG PIKE and RUFFIN ROAD

OPEN EVERY AFTERNOON AND ~~EVENING~~ *12 noon to 3 p.m.*

4th HOUSE ON RIGHT

The revised hours of operation are Mrs. Claudia D. Fonda's concession to neighborhood paranoia. There are church murmurs about cars coming and going all hours, rumors that the Fonda mattress is stuffed with ill-begotten dollars—or worse, talking horse as Biblical harbinger, modest Chesterfield the seat of imminent apocalypse.

Of course, for every doomsayer, there's another local who enjoys the horse's antics for what Mrs. Fonda says they are: entertainment. One voluble man-on-the-street, quoted in the July 18, 1927 *Richmond Times-Dispatch*, even declared Lady Wonder the heroine of her kind:

"In this age when horses have lost caste due to the automobile, she gets my respect. I mean, imagine a flivver telling you the square root of 81!"

***

Dr. Joseph Banks Rhine, a young botanist who history remembers dimly as "the father of parapsychology," is driving his Studebaker Dictator down the back roads of Chesterfield, Virginia. He has thick black eyebrows that bristle like terrified caterpillars and a wild-eyed urge to debunk something.

Dr. Rhine only became the father of parapsychology after he and his wife, Dr. Louisa Rhine, attended a public lecture titled "Proofs of Immortality," given in Chicago in 1922 by the author Sir Arthur Conan Doyle. The Rhines went for laughs, planning to mock the swooning matrons clutching their Sherlock omnibuses.

But when Sir Arthur intoned, with quavering ecstasy, that famed Boston medium Mina Crandon had channeled his dead son, spoken in his childlike voice, uttered his own innocent words, Dr. Rhine was blindsided by possibility. For he, like most scientists, existed in a state of perpetual longing, craving the rush of discovery. If there was even a seed of truth in what Sir Arthur (himself a medical man, an optometrist) swore was real, he told Louisa, ferreting out proof would be a worthier life's work than the pondscum and lichen that filled his lab hours. If the mind did indeed survive the body in a soul-like state, then they had to be separate entities. Dr. Rhine thought this division could be proven by confirming the existence of "extrasensory perception," which he defined as the acquisition of knowledge through non-physical means. Though Louisa had managed to talk him out of attending seminary, he found he still wanted to "do for religion something like what the germ theory did for medicine," and uncover the physical forces behind miracles.

Still, Dr. Rhine knew that for any positive ESP results to be considered, he must first cultivate a reputation of unimpeachable objectivity. Only by exposing hoaxes could he speak as an authority when actual paranormal phenomena occurred.

His crusade began when he co-authored an article with Dr. Louisa Rhine for the *Journal of Abnormal and Social Psychology*. Published in 1927, the Rhines' debut exposed the "teleplasmic hands" which oozed from Mina Crandon's nethers during her séances as bits of cow trachea, sewn into tentacular fingers by her accomplice husband and placed in her vagina ahead of time.

This triumph over charlatanism made international headlines. The sensation that followed made Sir Arthur Conan Doyle himself take out a full-page ad in the *Boston Herald* denouncing Dr. Joseph Banks Rhine as "a monumental ass." This backhanded endorsement of Dr. Rhine's objectivity cemented his reputation. Thus, the field of parapsychology was first plowed. Duke University added both Rhines to their psychology department, sheltering their upstart discipline under its well-funded wing.

At the Duke Parapsychology Lab, the Rhines conduct probability tests with dice and playing cards, searching for telepathy in curious student volunteers. Under Dr. Louisa Rhine's watch, several undergraduates have exhibited psychic abilities beyond mathematical chance. But the scientific community likes skeptics, not crusaders. Whenever Dr. Joseph Banks Rhine proves ESP's existence, his methodology is called to the carpet, and he is accused of the very chicanery he's famous for exposing. He is accused of sensory leakage, card counting, unconscious signals, tells, and cheats.

Alas, these fears are not unfounded. A knot of cardiganed co-eds from Dr. Joseph Banks Rhine's hypnotism class told him his ESP cards are a hit at parties, since in certain light you can easily see through to whatever shape is on the other side: red cross, blue circle, black square, green star. Dr. Rhine reminded them that all test subjects in his laboratory are isolated behind corkboard screens, unable to see the cards he holds, let alone look through them. He got so angry, he pounded his fist on the doorjamb of his office. His students told him to have a nice weekend and disappeared snickering down the hall.

***

What follows is a transcript of a conversation between Lady Wonder, equine oracle, and one Reverend Lloyd Parker, a God-fearing man from nearby Bellwood, Virginia. He mailed it to the Rhines' lab thirty times between 1925 and 1927, begging them to exorcise the beast.

"What is the date on this penny in my hand?"

"1-9-1-4"

"How do you like what you do?"

"D-O-N-T"

"Is my wife true to me?"

"A-R-E-Y-O-U"

"What do I have here in my pocket?"

"K-N-I-F-E"

"Would you like to be a human?"

"Y-E-S"

"How do you do it, Lady Wonder?"

"M-I-N-D"

***

Mrs. Claudia D. Fonda doesn't ride or drive, so Lady Wonder has never known the bovine heft of a saddle or tasted cold steel. A wedding present from her husband, Clarence, Mrs. Fonda's orphaned filly was bottle-fed and coddled on their parlor rug. As far as she's concerned, she's a dog or a person, so Lady was confused when she grew too big to fit through the Fondas' front door. They moved her into the pasture alongside the house. But Mrs. Fonda noticed the horse showed up whenever she thought of her, just as if she'd whistled. She'd be on the porch wringing laundry, think of Lady, and here she'd come cantering up from the fire pond, clods of earth flying in her hoofed wake.

Mrs. Fonda's kept Pomeranians since she was a girl, and she's always taught them tricks because "a dog likes a job." It was natural to wonder if Lady could learn something. Mrs. Fonda ordered a set of wooden alphabet blocks from the Sears catalogue and showed the filly how to spell simple words by turning them over with her nose: yes, no, horse, dog. Then she had Clarence build the typewriter/xylophone, and once Lady mastered that, they added "Wonder" to her name and hung out a shingle.

"But we've never made any claims," Mrs. Fonda concludes with a flourish.

Dr. Joseph Banks Rhine fidgets on the orange sofa, regarding the barn, which he'd imagined would look more like a fortuneteller's tent and less like a stable, gauzy drapery, drippy candles, the works. The horse stands half-asleep behind her strange alphabet, reminding him of a cow waiting to be milked.

"The Lady's an educated horse, is what we've always said. No more, no less," Mrs. Fonda tells him. "People ask her questions, what they do with the answers is their business, not mine. We make a little pin money here, not the millions people say. I don't open Sundays. And I turn away gamblers on moral principle—I want that in writing."

"I'm not here to shut you down, Mrs. Fonda. Only to observe and record."

"Is that what you told Mina Crandon?" she asks, tremulous.

"Well, Mina Crandon made claims," says Dr. Rhine.

Abashed, Mrs. Fonda sinks into her wing-backed chair and pats her lap, causing Pudgy the Pomeranian to abandon his kinderklavier. He has obediently plinked out "The Bells of St. Mary's" since Dr. Rhine's Studebaker Dictator motored up the drive.

"How shall we begin?" she asks, petting Pudgy.

Dr. Rhine says he'll start by seeing Lady Wonder perform as she usually would, as a control. Seeming relieved, Mrs. Fonda takes her place well behind the horse's left shoulder. She draws a ratty riding crop from an umbrella can welded to the typewriter/xylophone, then raises the business end to the level of her eyes to begin her usual pre-show patter. He may ask Lady Wonder three questions: tell her nothing, she tells all. Dr. Rhine clears his throat and looks the mare in the eye.

"What is two plus two?" he asks, feeling absurd.

Lady Wonder emits a low ungulate moan. Stirring, her massive triangular head weaves back and forth over the tin letters, the cups of her ears trained on Dr. Rhine, her goundy eyes rolling. Finally the mare lowers her flaring nostrils to the third row, where the digits are ranged 0 to 9. Her eyelids droop as she works whiskery lips around the lever that flips forth the 4. Then she nods, folding her wide tongue over itself with a vulgar slurp.

The whole act takes just under a minute. Once Lady Wonder has answered, Mrs. Fonda resets the typewriter/xylophone. There is no physical contact between them at any point. No treats or positive reinforcement are employed. But that was a softball question, Dr. Rhine reminds himself—he asked something others surely have before, as a warm up.

"What is the sum of eight and seven?" asks Dr. Rhine. This time he watches the woman, not the horse. Again, Mrs. Fonda's crop remains still while Lady Wonder sways over her array of letters, neck crooked like a dowsing rod. Finally she drops her nose to the number row to nudge forward the 1 and the 5.

Dr. Rhine clears his throat with authority, feigning disinterest.

"And what is my name?"

"R-I-N-E," spells Lady Wonder, roving among the keys with a typist's precision.

"Sometimes she neglects silent letters, especially with the H and the I so close together," apologizes Mrs. Fonda, rooting in her coat pocket for a carrot.

Lady Wonder paws and nods, baring calcareous teeth. She snatches the treat Mrs. Fonda offers and crunches down, spraying wet orange flecks on her mistress's coat. Dr. Rhine silently compares what he's just seen to a paper he reread in preparation for the occasion: Oskar Pfungst's 1907 report on the Clever Hans case, in which a German trotter appeared able to count, but was later found to be offering conditioned responses, cued by the trainer.

"She's remarkable, Mrs. Fonda," is what he says, though, because validation makes a subject feel at ease. "Will she answer again?"

"She will until she's tired," says Mrs. Fonda. "A horse has limits."

***

What follows is a selection of the 150 questions put to Lady Wonder, alleged equine clairvoyant, by Dr. Joseph Banks Rhine, father of parapsychology, between December 8th and 10th, 1928, in the Fonda barn outside of Chesterfield, Virginia.

It is worth noting that, had Dr. Rhine paid the going rate for the mare's services during this inquisition, Mrs. Claudia D. Fonda would have made enough to order an ermine coat from the 1928 Sears-Roebuck catalog.

"Spell doctor as I've written it here."

"D-O-K-T-O-R"

"Who was our first President?"

"W-A-S-H-I-N-G-T-O N"

"And what have I written down here?"

"M-E-S-O-P-O-T-A-M-I-A"

"And here?"

"H-I-N-D-U-S-T-A-N"

"And here?"

"C-A-R-O-L-I-N-A"

"Who will win the next election?"

"H-A-R-D-I-N-G"

"Again?"

"Y-E-S"

"How did I get here today?"

"E-N-G-I-N-E"

"What time is it?"

"D-I-N-N-E-R"

***

According to Dr. Rhine's field notes, several variables changed throughout his interrogation of Lady Wonder. For a time, he had one of his corkboard dividers placed before the horse, to prevent Mrs. Fonda from reading the answers he wrote in his notebook. Lady Wonder did not falter. Next he removed the woman's riding crop, which she relinquished with a smile. The mare's answers remained mostly correct, and witty when they weren't, even with Mrs. Fonda's hands crossed behind her back.

After several wrong answers in a row, Mrs. Fonda would say Lady was getting tired, or hungry, or mareish, and turn her loose for a gallop and a roll in the pasture. At first Dr. Rhine thought this was a cover for the animal's stubborn disobedience of hidden commands. But as the process continued, he too grew to note the mare's changeable moods—an irritated flick of the ear, hind leg cocked to kick the wall.

Dr. Rhine's field notes from the Lady Wonder case are written in a sober hand. What they don't record is how his heart leapt as each correct letter tumbled forward, again and again, beyond the vicissitudes of chance. Like a stalagmite, his belief accreted with each question. Still, one variable remained.

On the third and final day of his investigation, Dr. Rhine asked Mrs. Fonda if she would leave the barn, so he could rule out the possibility of signaling between woman and horse once and for all. He expected the horsewife to resist with a carnival barker's dodge, calculated to ensure the show could go on. Instead Mrs. Fonda agreed to go up to the house, saying she wanted to start fixing lunch anyhow.

"I'll be in the kitchen if the Lady needs me," she told him, cool as gin.

Surprised to overcome her, Dr. Rhine considered his plan of attack. Lady Wonder seemed unaffected by her mistress's departure, bored even, snuffling her nose along the edge of the typewriter/xylophone. Drawing near, he gazed into the brown syrup of her eyes and found his own face reflected there, bent, as though seen in a spoon.

"Lady Wonder," he intoned, "What is my wife's name?"

Stirring, Lady Wonder roved over the first row of her typewriter/xylophone. As she moved she watched her guest, who held his breath when she dropped to the second tier of tin letters to hover above the L. It seemed right to give the horse every chance to succeed, so Dr. Rhine pictured his beloved as he'd first seen her: skimming duckweed off an aquarium in the graduate botany lab. He saw Louisa's mauve high heels perched on the stepstool she used to reach the tank. He saw Louisa's crooked grin as she turned to say hello. He stared at Lady Wonder until his vision swam, the six letters in Louisa a mantra in his mind, a cheerleader chant.

Satisfied somehow, Lady Wonder brought her nose down hard on the L, flipping it forward with a decisive snap. The O and the U she found faster, but switching rows to choose the letter I seemed to throw off her rhythm. Lady Wonder paused, tongue slurping against corn-colored teeth, watching Dr. Rhine as if she wanted something from him. Then she doubled back to bump the E, spelling "L-O-U-I-E."

This was his private nickname for Louisa, something the horse couldn't know on its own.

Dr. Rhine leapt to his feet, giddy with possibility, aflame with eureka.

***

In a tea-toned photograph taken at the conclusion of Dr. Rhine's 1928 visit to the Fonda family farm in Chesterfield, Virginia, Lady Wonder and Mrs. Fonda stand framed before a canvas tent, their coats bathed in white winter sun. The father of parapsychology himself is behind the lens. He has tossed his hat aloft to make Lady Wonder turn to face the camera: ears quirked alert, white blaze aglow.

Mrs. Fonda is radiant, wearing nylons and Mary Janes despite the barnyard mud, a wool cloche hugging her dark curls. While Lady Wonder watches Dr. Rhine's hat hurtle back to earth, Mrs. Fonda proudly grins at her fuzzy cheek. She is smiling in this photograph because she has just learned that Dr. Rhine, famed debunker of Mina Crandon's vaginal hand, destroyer of livelihoods, really believes her pet horse is psychic.

Or, as he later wrote in the *Journal of Parapsychology*: "There appear to be no loopholes, no reasonable possibility of signaling, either of a conscious or unconscious character. There is left only the telepathic explanation, the transference of mental influence by an unknown process. Nothing was discovered that failed to accord with it, and no other hypothesis seems tenable in view of the results."

These claims made Dr. Rhine the laughingstock of the discipline he created, which is quite an achievement. Fringe science supported the search for ESP in human beings, but telepathy in a dumb horse? Absurd. Undeterred, Dr. Rhine continued to claim positive cases of extrasensory perception and psychokinesis in the Duke student body well into the 1970s. However, none of his experiments were ever successfully reproduced outside his lab, and several of the Rhines' graduate assistants were found to be botching results, having seen the cards and dice and thought it was all a game.

Apologists like to read the father of parapsychology's final decline as an about face—evidence that as the separation of his own body and soul drew near, a necessary skepticism crept into him. Some titles among Dr. Rhine's late papers do hint at a cowed repentance: "Security Versus Deception in Parapsychology," "How *Does* One Decide About ESP?" and lastly, "Parapsychology: A Correction."

The truth is, Dr. Rhine's mind so commingled science and religion that, for him, denying the existence of ESP meant admitting there were no souls to ascend to heaven. His faith in the Lord was as absolute as his confirmation bias. Indeed, they were one and the same. This is why, sitting on an orange floral sofa in a Chesterfield, Virginia backyard barn, he leapt right to thinking God had walked through the room.

Raised in the automotive era, Dr. Rhine had no concept of a horse's state of mind. Having never ridden, he didn't know that a rattling leaf can jolt a whole herd into a blind stampede or understand how a mount tenses under a nervous rider, searching for the threat signaled by their breath and legs and voice. Mrs. Fonda had simply trained Lady Wonder to aim this natural anxiety at the customer. Each time the mare swayed serpentine over her typewriter/xylophone, she read subtle changes in her interviewers' respiration, scent, and body language as she neared each longed-for letter—a held breath, a whiff of sweat, a fist knuckled into the orange sofa, rigid with anticipation. The more a person wanted to believe in Lady Wonder, the better she spelled. Thus Dr. Joseph Banks Rhine, a man always already waiting for the stone to roll away, was an ideal subject.

Other images of Lady Wonder, equine sphinx, remain. Nearly all depict the mare alongside Mrs. Claudia D. Fonda, at various stages of their long career in backyard showbiz. Together they sustained the Fonda fortunes long after Clarence was injured at work, Mrs. Fonda the breadwinner in an era when most women weren't allowed to be.

The last few photos of the two, taken for *LIFE* magazine in the 1950s, depict a puffy Mrs. Fonda and a swaybacked Lady, the woman's riding crop held aloft as the raggedy mare spells Y-E-S on her old typewriter/xylophone. These were taken after Lady Wonder allegedly channeled Leroy Baker, a missing three-year-old boy. When questioned by police, the horse spelled out "P-I-T-T-S-F-I-E-L-D-W-A-T-E-R-W-H-E-E-L." The child's waterlogged body was eventually found in the Field-Wilde quarry, which was a kind of pit with water in it, according to Mrs. Fonda. Later, she refused to let her aged pet name the boy's killer, declaring Lady Wonder retired from public investigation.

"You can't use the word of a horse to accuse anybody of a crime," said Mrs. Fonda, in her last printed statement on Lady Wonder. "Besides, we've never made any claims."

THE LOST HOOF OF FIRE HORSE #12

THE HOOF

"No hoof, no horse," horse people say, tucking each leg between their knees, fingers scanning for cracks in the keratin, bad pasterns, or thick rings of bone. This quadripartite handshake has continued for 5,500 years—a ritual repeated throughout each animal's lifetime, verdict changing with time and care.

But here there is no horse, just hoof—the left hind leg of a half-Percheron mare, to be precise, dead since March 1890. Trotted out for photographs, the lost hoof of fire horse #12 rests on spotless cotton as Smithsonian interns Instagram it into the datasphere, now reaching white gloves into frame, now turning the artifact gently toward the light. Its black preservative coating glistens like wet licorice under the fluorescent hum.

Stabled in a metal cabinet at the National Museum of Natural History's archives for more than a century, the lost hoof of fire horse #12 has a drawer all to itself, filed between ambergris and mammoth teeth. Its final shoe remains attached by a lone nail, the black metal U torqued ninety degrees away from where the farrier nailed it on, now become a C. Three other nails tore through the hoof wall, dislodged by velocity, while friction bent the two remaining back against the shoe, tips jabbed accusingly at the holes they flew from, leaving dark dents in the corium. Cauterized at the ankle soon after its retrieval from the streets of our nation's flammable capital, the hoof was dunked, shoe and all, in black gutta-percha for safekeeping: a gory candy apple.

The uniformity of the severed limb's tarry coating somewhat softens its surgical horror. This was District Fire Chief R.W. Dutton's first thought upon receiving the finished *objet d'art*, wrapped in butcher paper inside a wooden crate and smelling strongly of molten rubber. His second thought, after it was unpacked onto his desk, was that the lost hoof of fire horse #12 would make an intriguing paperweight; something for reporters and government officials to mention whenever they visited his office.

He was right. Whenever anyone came to see him, Chief Dutton launched into a stump speech about the marvelous fidelity of the horses in his employ. Eyes welling, he'd explain how this hoof was amputated alive from its noble owner in the line of duty—how that incredible horse galloped eight more blocks on the bloody stump left behind, so pure was its desire to save humans from four-alarm hellfire. Once his listeners were groping for handkerchiefs, Chief Dutton artfully segued into an explanation of why the department needed upwards of seventy head per annum, to replace those unfortunate horses who gave all and asked so little in return.

"A steam engine won't die to save your life," Chief would intone, gaveling the hoof on stacked ledgers for emphasis. "A fire horse will."

Thus the lost hoof of fire horse #12 filled municipal coffers for years upon years, tax dollars buying colt upon colt to fling at the greedy flames.

But removed from the long-gone context of Chief Dutton's desk, the lost hoof of fire horse #12 does not curate neatly. For over a century now, it has, like so much American detritus, been deemed worthy of preservation but not display. Unlike the gawping coyotes and pickled squids in the National Museum of Natural History's collection, which having died whole, are shown so, a lone hoof can't be shoehorned into a timeline about evolution or blend unobtrusively into a Great Plains diorama. It turns out that dismemberment requires a longer explanation than what fits on a standard museum label. The lost hoof of fire horse #12 demands its own vitrine, alcove, and motion-sensitive spotlight, all luxuries the Smithsonian Institution cannot spare in the age of interactive edutainment.

In truth, the hoof has never been family-friendly. The earliest recorded evidence of its presence at the National Museum of Natural History appears in a May 1902 *Washington Post* article titled "STORY OF AN EQUINE HERO. Famous Run of Fire Engine Horse to Be Perpetuated." In this short item, Professor Samuel Pierpont Langley, renowned aviator and third Secretary of the Smithsonian Institution, tactfully rejects Chief Dutton's request that the hoof be placed on permanent public display.

"At some future time it might be thought best to place on exhibition a case of objects illustrating the work of the fire department, when it would, of course, be proper to include the hoof," avers Langley, taking pains to praise the "wonderful endurance" of the animal, and concede its demise indeed "one of the incidents of the history of the horse which deserved to be preserved."

Chief Dutton, who was by that point more interested in acquiring a herd of steam-powered fire engines than perpetuating the useful myth of the loyal fire horse, accepted Langley's refusal without protest. Thus his macabre paperweight was first consigned to "the nation's attic," which is really a basement, attics being notoriously bad places to preserve anything.

THE HORSE

City records detail that this particular fire horse #12 pulled the No. 3 Company's second hose-cart from August 1887 to March 1890, a short but average tenure for the high-risk career of a sentient urban emergency vehicle.

Hand-selected at auction by Chief Dutton, this #12 was a compact gray half-Percheron mare with a docked tail, chopped short at the root soon after birth. Besides being sufficiently fancy for parades, gray horses were easier for pedestrians to spot in the dark, when engines hurtled top speed through gaslit streets toward distant flames. Chief Dutton liked to keep the capital city's herd at around two hundred head, since it wasn't unusual to lose a few horses each month to disease, lameness, colic, or some other infirmity.

On average, just one out of twenty horses made the grade, and even these couldn't take the strain of service for more than a decade or so. If sound, some had second careers pulling omnibuses or delivery carts. But fire horse training was a deep spell, carved hard. Newspapers across the country regularly reported retirees bolting at the distant clang of station bells, completely forgetting the poor milkmen behind the reins in their mad, moth-like dash toward the flames.

It took a rare one. A fire horse had to stand motionless, flight instinct overridden, as its harness was lowered from the dark rafters, then strapped across its trembling chest.

Next the double door was flung wide, launching the blinkered teams into the cobbled streets, wheels tipping around corners and brass fittings flashing, the horses' trust utterly vested in the shouting driver who aimed them, galloping, toward smoke and fire.

For #12 that was Jack Knox, a good-hearted young fellow with a face like a shovel. During the long hours when buildings weren't on fire, #12 dozed with him in her stall. While clean, the stable of No. 3 Engine Company was a far cry from the ideal equine habitat painted behind the Smithsonian's prairie diorama, with its amber waves of grain in the middle distance, smudged mustangs' triangular heads bent earthward in greedy supplication. Fire horse #12, a.k.a. "Queenie," was well kept, by the standards then accepted for urban livestock. Knox saw to it that her bedding was dry; she received ample salt, oats and hay, and a walk around the block on days the engines didn't run.

But cities give animals strange ideas; limn instinct with odd impulse. For example, fire horse #12 spooked at any tree taller than the caged sidewalk saplings she was used to galloping past. Simultaneously, she was known to doze unfazed near raging infernos while hot sparks rained upon her white-starred face.

The fire that killed #12 was four-alarm, with long orange geysers of flame spouting from the attic of a brick tenement like an infernal crown. Escaped tenants stood aloof across the street, swaddled babies in full squall as the crowd watched the No. 3 Engine joust the blaze. It was an average disaster, blamed on a drunkard with a lit pipe on a horsehair mattress. The unintentional arsonist was the only casualty besides fire horse #12, shot at the scene after Jack Knox found his charge hopping in the gutter on just three good legs.

"To be viewed as reliable by the public," said Chief Dutton, presiding over the shell-shocked company back at the station, "our fair capital's fire horses must appear an infinite herd, a unified faceless machine, ever ready to renew itself, like the army or the police. Sentimentality endangers confidence. Instead of eulogizing one horse, let us all be grateful that tonight, Death spared us all."

There followed a moment of silence that lasted exactly as long as it took for the No. 3 Company to realize Chief Dutton was finished talking. He took his time ascending the stairs to his office, pausing several times for gravitas. Then someone whooped, cards and beer emerged, and Jack Knox realized he was expected to pass the wee hours toasting a fire well doused, as though no great tragedy had occurred, as though he hadn't begun each morning for the past three years by pressing his cheek against Queenie's broad belly to listen for the secret aquarium of her gut. He could not unhear its healthy gurgle, or the toothy clash of cobblestone on bone. He could not unsee the meaty insides of her left hind as he shrouded her for the knackers, tarpaulin flapping in the breeze.

He remembered Queenie and her hitch partner, King, snorting as nightcapped citizens clung to doorways to watch the hose-cart clatter past. As usual, Knox had leaned into the corners, balanced half-crouched behind his surging team, traces flying. He never slowed, or pulled up, or took notice of Queenie's injury beyond the awful observation that she was dragging somewhat, which made him drive her harder. There was only room in his throbbing head for *fire* and *faster* and *go*.

It stands to reason that losing an entire hoof from the fetlock down should make a horse limp or scream or collapse under itself, but Queenie ran on—she was just that brave or dumb or terrified.

THE HOOF

The death of fire horse #12 reads like the noble sacrifice Chief Dutton wanted it remembered as until one realizes, as Knox must have, that the mare *couldn't* have stopped galloping even if she'd wanted to, yoked as she was to King.

Picture the appendage wedged upright between the trolley rails, shinbone a stick in a steel river. That's how Knox, unintentional prince of this morbid equestrian Cinderella, expected to find the lost hoof of fire horse #12. Given the preserved hoof's appearance today, it is more likely that Queenie's horseshoe got caught between the rail and the planking, after which the centrifugal force of the team's unstoppable gallop resulted in spontaneous amputation.

What's clear is how fast (by 19th century standards) the death of fire horse #12 became a topic of national debate. In an April 1890 editorial reprinted nationwide, minor newspaper magnate and self-proclaimed "wild, woolly Westerner," T. E. Goodrich of Shelbyville, Indiana, heaped "shame upon Washington" on the maltreated mare's behalf.

"An 'equine hero' indeed was that horse, but what of the man who had him shot? What of a city government that would permit such an act?" wrote Goodrich, with the armchair confidence distance affords. "Here in the 'Wild Woolly West,' an animal so faithful, so true, so noble as the poor beast your fire department slaughtered after it had performed a service never equaled, would have had its wound bandaged, healed, and made as near perfect as possible: then, in place of blowing its brains out, it would have been furnished comfortable quarters for the remainder of its life. An intelligent people hang their heads in shame to think such a deed would ever be thought of in the Capital City of the grandest country God ever blessed."

Given the sheer number of broken-down ponies shot throughout the American West, Goodrich's words are obvious hyperbole. His manic screed does, however, suggest why Chief Dutton had his curious paperweight entombed at the Smithsonian Institution in 1902—twelve years after the rest of #12 was buried—instead of chucking the hoof once it, like the horse, had outlived usefulness. Dutton knew trying to honor the relic in some official capacity was more politic than dealing with people like T. E. Goodrich inquiring as to its whereabouts.

Though the hoof of fire horse #12 appears solid and uniform from the outside, while alive it encapsulated a dozen interconnected anatomical structures, which in turn nourished a host of opportunistic bacteria and fungi. The horse's evolution from multi-toed quadruped to single-toed ungulate is a popular museum subject, as ample fossil records exist for all known iterations of the equine appendage, revealing how the last toe slid upward over millennia, then shrunk into the dime-sized discs of keratin still seen on the inner thighs of *equus caballus*. The remaining digits fused, cornifying into layers of outer wall and inner capsule that could be seen even now if the desiccated hoof of fire horse #12 were sawn in half, like an Easter ham.

Each hoof is a calendar recording winter and spring, famine and feast, its structure as profoundly affected by moisture as the rolling grasslands it evolved to tread. Too much rain lets thrush fester in the clefts. Drought leads to contraction and sandcracks. Knowing this as everyone did in horse-powered America, the drivers of No. 3 Engine Company performed strengthening rituals based on science and superstition alike. They painted on neatsfoot oil, a pale-yellow unguent made by boiling cows' feet until they liquefy, hoof for a hoof. Witch hazel and arnica were rubbed into fetlocks. Pulverized shells from the local oyster den got stirred into bran mash.

Jack Knox's own tender podiatry remains evident today, as the lost hoof of fire horse #12 sports the smooth groove of a phonograph record, strong rings of horn accreted monthly. Read like a palm, the hoof's surface indicates that up until that last awful second, the horse attached to it was well fed and cared for, maybe even a little bit loved.

THE HORSE

Jack Knox couldn't rescue fire horse #12, so he saved her hoof instead. His reasons for doing this are murky. Maybe he had to return the appendage to the station to forgive himself for not driving the whole horse back. Maybe he wanted to show his fellow hose-cart drivers exactly how trolley tracks could mangle a good animal, warn them against getting too cocky behind the reins. Regardless of his motivations, surely "interesting paperweight" wasn't Knox's immediate intention when he first snatched the lost hoof of fire horse #12 out of the gutter and tucked it, damp and bloody, under his coat.

Imagine the Chief's horrorstruck expression when Knox plonked the hoof onto his desk papers like a butcher's bone, a gauntlet, a dare. Such devotion made tossing it down the rubbish chute a non-option. Keeping it was the only fair answer. So in the end Chief Dutton ended up having to save fire horse #12, too, whether he wanted to or not, and so did Professor Samuel Pierpont Langley of the Smithsonian Institution, and so do its white-gloved interns, and so do we, breathing at a glowing hoof on a computer screen.

If souls are real and horses have them, then it's nice to think how the soul of fire horse #12 might still be attached to her leftover hoof, tethered to it like a metaphysical balloon. Even in her spectral state, the gray mare might relish the dark silence of her subterranean tomb, or at least find it familiar.

After all, in life she was used to being stored, stowed, and saved for later—for that is what it was to be stabled in the basement box stalls of No. 3 Engine Company, forever edgy for the bell.

SHOOTING
A MULE

"It became necessary, one day, at Willet's Point, to destroy a worthless mule, and the subject was made the occasion of giving useful instruction to the military class there stationed." —from *Scientific American*, September 24, 1881.

Dicky keeps saying that things could have gone differently if that damned fool mule had had the good sense not to cow-kick General Abbot in the thigh this Thursday last. A barrel of salt pork could easily have been pressed into service, or a side of rotting beef, but no, that rotten mule had to go and assault a commanding officer, and so, Dicky reckoned, he had to pay.

"See, a *horse* would have shown some respect," he said, crooking his mouth to spit. "But once you start putting donkey in there, it's just *unnatural*, the creature's instincts get all mixed up, it starts getting its own ideas about who's boss, against God's plan, and I tell you what, that's a dangerous thing." He ground his spit into the ruddy dirt with his bootheel, and nodded vigorously as he reached for his snuff. "It'll get just what it deserves, and I tell you, I'm sure going to watch."

He was. But then, we all were. General Abbot's vendetta against "Colonel," the mid-aged grade mule that had left him with a bruise shaped like a cannonball, was already the stuff of legend around our battalion, and the General's revenge was, if Dicky's account of the matter was to be believed, destined for epic scale. The General was a ruthless man at best, and the old Colonel's assault, prompted by a cinch pulled too tight, had invoked his purest wrath. That afternoon, he subjected us to hours of calisthenics under the New York summer sun. He trampled the already suffering scrub grass of the parade ground, all the while slapping a riding crop against his bad thigh, as if to prolong the pain, and through it, stoke the steaming engine of his rage.

By evening, during an impromptu dinner party at Corporal Smith's palatial manse, the beast's fate was sealed. The execution was imminent, and the secret method employed would, we heard, be a modern wonder worthy of Barnum himself, a spectacular of American know-how. Dicky began collecting bets at sundown, weighing the odds of electrocution versus firing squad, his eyes two thin slits in his leathern face as Henry, Thom, and all my chums invented novel ways to die.

But even the condemned should receive last rites. And that, it seemed, was left to me. I stole from my bed in the pitch of night, while my bunkmates snored on, unaware. I made my way to the stable softly. The horses were whales in the dark, silently shifting through the black, their massive bodies drifting just above the earth as they cropped the dewy brown grass. Not a soul was in sight, save them. And I was frightened as one is frightened in church. I, who had thrown rocks at them mere days before, drunk on cider with Dicky and Thom.

The mule I found alone, sequestered in a round pen beside the main barn, his great bullish head butting up against an empty feed drum, his huge brown eyes limpid, innocent of the drama that now surrounded him. He greedily lipped the handfuls of grass that I pushed through the fence, and allowed me to groom the long black funnels of his ears, stretching his neck out so I could scratch them. We smoked my last pipe of Cavendish together, that mule and I. And he seemed glad for the companionship of a fellow creature, however unfamiliar, his damp nostrils flaring and huffing, his warm breath joining coils of smoke.

As reveille sounded next morning, we were visited by the General himself. He marched through our bunkhouse, a wide grin slashing his bearded face, his best riding crop beating a tattoo upon his massive right thigh. A mincing, suited businessman brought up the rear, his shoulders burdened with an array of leather satchels, his forehead slick with perspiration despite the chill of the room. We dressed with rapidity and scrambled to attention.

"Today, boys, you will bear witness to history," announced General Abbot, his crop thwacking the footboard of Dicky's bed so hard, the metal rang out. My bowels crept at the sound. "With the technological assistance of my new acquaintance, this Englishman, Mr. Charles Bennett, I shall perform a grand experiment in the new art of—" and here the General looked to Bennett, who prompted him with a wormlike twist of the lips "—*instantaneous photography*, the likes of which the world has never known, and never shall again."

We were forthwith trooped out of the bunkhouse, unwashed and unbreakfasted, to a barren tract of land just south of the parade ground. There stood the Colonel, motionless and trusting, his rope tied securely to a wooden stake freshly driven into the earth. A makeshift surcingle secured around his girth was, we saw, elaborately attached to a host of electrical wires running through the dirt.

Upon our arrival, Bennett immediately rushed toward a tripod that straddled the land like a strange metal insect. The General boldly strode toward a card table ranged approximately thirty feet away from the beast, and we followed like puppies, jostling one another to take our places on either side of him, hastily buttoning our jackets and trousers. The table held a gadget I'd never seen before, and the General stood with one hand on either side of it, as if protecting the mysterious machinery from our prying eyes. We watched, puzzled, as Bennett approached the animal, accompanied by a petty officer who gentled it with a whiff of ether whilst a necklace of wire and gunnysacks was fastened about its noble neck. The daguerreotypist spoke then, his accent clipped and purposeful.

"The experiment will proceed as follows. The slide of my camera is supported by a fuse; this fuse and the payload attached to the subject are connected in the same electrical circuit, arranged by my assistant. On General Abbot's signal, an electrical pulse shall travel through the wiring, simultaneously activating the explosives and dropping my camera's slide, capturing the very second of detonation on one of my patented Instantaneous Gelatine Photographic Plates for all posterity."

The mule's vast ears flicked toward the sound of Bennett's voice, then toward Dicky, who was the first to applaud. And I stood at war with myself, scarcely believing where I was, the plain words "explosives" and "payload" ringing in my ears. The mule knew by scent that I, too, was here and frightened, bridling against my years of conditioning to remain behind the card table, shoulders back, chin up, until ordered otherwise. But then—

"Fire!" shouted the General, his hammy hands slamming down upon the device in front of him. And in a terrible instant, head was ejected from body, its momentary flight filling the air with a bloody mist until both portions of the animal fell to the ground, still. The General strode jauntily toward the steaming carcass, first lifting the beast's belly with the toe of his boot, then, with a broad smile, doffing his hat in the direction of the triumphant daguerreotypist, who excitedly exclaimed that, since all his equipment had worked as planned, we could soon expect him to publish an image of the headless creature, still standing, before the body had time to fall.

That evening, over cigars, Dicky declared the whole affair a delicious success, great sport and supremely edifying for all involved, particularly the mule. He said he couldn't wait for the photograph.

Later, silent in my bunk, I wondered if he and I had seen the same thing.

STOCK
FOOTAGE

Miss Lucille Mulhall
Roping Wild
Mexican Cattle,
the only woman in the world
accomplishing this dangerous feat.

In this movie a steer (wild, Mexican) bursts into the upper left corner of the screen just after the intertitle fades from view. It is pursued by Miss Lucille Mulhall, rancher Zachary Mulhall's blonde daughter, a woman known as "Queen of the Western Prairie," "Female Conqueror of Beef and Horn," and "The Lassoer in Lingerie," about which she publicly blushes. The steer runs along a split-rail fence that cuts frame neatly in half, creating a horizon line immediately broken by Miss Lucille, who rides a dark horse that hugs the rail as if this is Churchill Downs, and not the Miller Brothers' 101 Ranch outside Ponca City, Oklahoma. The steer has a head start, but Miss Lucille is gaining on him, white lasso whirling high over her head as her horse homes in, all three animals barreling toward the camera in a flipbook blur of hat and legs and hide.

While this is happening two women wearing nurses' caps move to stand in the background, we assume for the safety of Miss Lucille, who wings her *reata* around the steer's horns so lightly, it's hard to see that she's won until the animal is yanked neck-first away from the fence. The flimsy wire dips dangerously toward the camera under the corn-fed weight of it, and we remember that Miss Lucille has wrung a few necks out of sheer enthusiasm, snapping her rope too tight.

Cut to Miss Lucille and her horse pursuing another steer, this one white with a black head, as if it's been dunked in ink. The camera has been turned to follow Miss Lucille's approach from the opposite side of the arena. There's a disorienting splice in the reel before her lariat slides under the critter's hooves, and when the image resolves the camera has moved again. The background is now dominated by what looks like a grandstand of waving spectators, but upon closer inspection turns out to be a rocky butte, animated by heat in the air. Snagged around the heels by Miss Lucille, the second steer folds like a lawn chair. Our heroine leaps from her backing horse and swoops toward the prone bovine in one confident motion. She winds her waxed rope around the steer's bony ankles, then leaps up looking for the camera, her empty hands thrust overhead in triumph before she wanders off-screen, unaware that the cameraman is bad at panning.

Left to his own devices, Miss Lucille's roping horse stretches the lasso tight between its saddle and the steer, chewing the bit as he backs. The steer gathers its bound legs into a wobbly tripod and scrambles to its feet. But Miss Lucille marches back, running her hand along the rope as she rejoins her horse, and the steer flops back into the dirt, defeated.

Fade to a medium shot of Miss Lucille aboard a different horse, identifiable to the discerning horseman by the telltale white stocking on his right hind. It is as if the filmmaker—an Edison man—decided that we deserved a better look at our prairie rose, or perhaps he assumes his audience harbors the same doubts as the gentlemen who tore her shirt at Madison Square Garden, exposing her breasts in a bid to prove the Queen of the Saddle was a man.

But this new horse doesn't want to play along, and neither does Miss Lucille. Her mouth twists into a grimace as she dutifully gathers her lasso and urges her colt back into the center of the frame. She barks something at the cameraman, her face a white smear bobbing around under a gray hat, then lets the coiled lariat fall to her hip, as if posing for a photograph—but her colt lurches forward, ruining the tableau. At first he seems to be running away with her, but Miss Lucille grins as they gallop past the camera, and we know she told him to misbehave.

Miss Lucille and
Manager C. L. Harris
In Bliss, Oklahoma

Someone has scribbled in grease pencil on the film leader, producing an illegible flash of black lines that moves vertically over the screen as the sprocket holes rattle through the projector. Then Miss Lucille and Manager C. L. Harris are standing together in front of a rocky outcropping in Bliss, Oklahoma. In the middle distance a line of well-dressed cowboys parade toward the left side of the frame. But back to Miss Lucille and Manager C. L. Harris, who face the camera, awaiting a signal.

Dressed in a gleaming white shirtwaist and fringed split skirt, Miss Lucille fastens her hands to her hips, fingertips pointing at her nether regions. It is a resting posture she subconsciously adopted during long days out on her father's range, roping and riding alongside rough men who hoped she'd notice their crotches. Manager C.L. Harris holds his arms crossed behind him, in a position widely understood by anthropologists to mean that he is insecure about his authority over the situation, or perhaps anxious about how he is being perceived. His watch chain is hooked to his waistcoat. His Stetson sets high on his forehead, and he looks too clean, like he showers at hotels. Both Manager C.L. Harris and Miss Lucille look worried all of a sudden. This is because they just saw the cameraman duck behind his machine, and realized that they can no longer take any cues from his eyes or expression.

But someone off-camera must say something, or wave, because now

Miss Lucille and Manager C.L. Harris turn stiffly toward each other, like Dutch children kissing in a clock. Miss Lucille seizes Manager C.L. Harris's right hand with her left. He removes his hat with his free hand, revealing the striking whiteness of his bare scalp, and places it over his heart like a good American. Of course, Miss Lucille and Manager C.L. Harris already know one another well, so it is unclear why they are shaking hands, though they exchange a few awkward words as they do so, keeping their faces turned toward the camera.

The handshake itself is firm and theatrical, lasting a half-second too long. It is exactly the kind of handshake that lends real credence to the rumor that Miss Lucille and Manager C.L. Harris's relationship may go beyond the promotional. She is famously undomesticated, a quality resulting in no fewer than two divorces, the quiet appearance of a baby "sister" at the Mulhall ranch, and a baby son at her ex-in-laws' St. Louis home, forgotten like a hankie or a toothbrush. We see Miss Lucille move her left hand onto Manager C.L. Harris's right shoulder and guide him toward the camera in a manner that suggests she is used to coaching his body. Then, as if remembering herself, she sways herself away from him, scratches her upper lip with her empty ring finger and fixes her gray eyes on something in the unknowable distance.

Manager C. L. Harris—grinning, oblivious—replaces his hat, and Miss Lucille Mulhall cuffs his shoulder again, leaning into him, telling him maybe she's done being filmed. She is strangely entreating now, almost shy, as if the girl within her has taken the reins. They approach the camera together, linking arms just after they think they're off-screen, but a few frames before they actually are.

Iva Park,
Queen of the Roundup,
presenting Miss Mulhall
with bouquet of flowers.

No reason is given as to why, but this movie features Iva Park: Queen of the Roundup cantering into the arena on a flashy paint to deliver a bouquet to Miss Lucille Mulhall, Queen of the Western Prairie, presumably at the behest of Manager C.L. Harris, who, as a modern American, is a sucker for any stunt that resembles the passing of a torch, or the replacement of the old with the new.

Miss Iva Park casually interrupts Miss Lucille's demonstration aboard her *haute école* horse, "Eddie C.," who holds one ivory foreleg outstretched and trembling, as if pointing at something in the dirt. Iva's little paint—a fine horse under any other circumstances—looks downright shabby next to the majestic Eddie C., who gleams like he's carved from marble, even when he's pinning his ears and setting his teeth. Eddie C. is unhappy about how quickly Iva Park and her paint slid in alongside him, without fanfare or warning. He does not like how close this strange horse's body is to his, and so he is reluctant to draw his hoof back to himself, even after his mistress asks him to do so several times, first with her leg, then her rein, then her voice.

If Miss Lucille is embarrassed or flustered by Eddie C.'s unusual hesitation, we do not know it, because her head and Iva Park's are decapitated at the top of the shot, just above their shoulders. The cameraman makes no attempt to adjust focus, perhaps due to the immense physical effort involved in moving his machine, which at this point in history weighs several hundred pounds, and as established in earlier sequences, cannot pan worth a damn.

So beheaded Miss Iva Park is presenting guillotined Miss Lucille Mulhall with a lovely bouquet, like the intertitle promised she would. The headless women stretch across the small gulf separating their horses, who express their mutual disdain with flared nostrils and whitening eyes. Miss Lucille shifts her reins into her left hand and graciously accepts a spray of black greenery and gray carnations with her right, all prettily wrapped in a white paper cone.

Now Eddie C. is prancing backwards, because his monocular vision did not allow him to see what was passed onto his back, and he is convinced that it could be a mountain lion. Iva Park's little paint horse executes a tight pivot on its hindquarters. The cowgirl keeps her black-gloved arm outstretched throughout this maneuver, her palm upturned. As a result, we find ourselves watching her instead of Miss Lucille, who bows over Eddie C.'s neck, lifting the flowers to her nose in the universal gesture of bouquet reception. An irritated Eddie C. is also made to bow, tucking his head against his chest and folding his left hoof into the dirt while maintaining the extension in his right leg. The horse flicks his ears forward, comforted for a moment by doing something familiar. The camera lurches up and to the left to get Eddie C.'s whole body into the frame, raising further questions about its operator's continuing decision to cut the riders' heads off-screen.

Iva Park and her paint have not completely exited the arena, because someone waved for them to pose beside Miss Lucille, and here they are again. Meanwhile—unnoticed by both cowgirls, who have their hands full with flowers and reins and two horses who honestly dislike each other—Miss Lucille's famous miniature bronco, "Tiny Mite," has wandered into the right side of the frame. Tiny Mite is at liberty to do as he pleases, so he flattens his ears and bares his teeth at the larger horses, who rear and plunge in terror, their tails waving like angry flags while their headless riders' legs flap behind tooled leather *tapaderos*.

Cow Girl Race.
Accident—Miss Iva Park,
Queen of the Roundup,
Injured

In this movie, someone (C. L. Harris?) has decided to stage a galloping race between Miss Iva Park and Miss Lucille Mulhall. A few other cowgirls have been invited to fortify the competition, but nobody roots for them but their sweethearts, and anyway, the winner doesn't matter, now that we anticipate disaster.

All five riders are ranged parallel across an extreme long shot, waiting for the starter's gun. Both Miss Iva Park and Miss Lucille are astride nondescript bays, though this is not immediately apparent due to the continuing presence of Miss Iva Park's paint, now being ridden by a woman far less skilled than she. There are two false starts as the overeager horse breaks formation, charging ahead of the pack as if stuck with a hot poker. We view both gallops in rapid succession, because the filmmaker has thoughtfully trimmed out the awkward half-minute or so that it took for the horse to circle the track and return to the starting line.

When the paint has kicked up enough dust to engulf the remaining horses' knees, Miss Iva Park, hollering, scratches him from the race. The paint gallops off screen a third time, then they're off—springing forward at the unheard gun, Miss Lucille Mulhall is on the outside, Miss Iva Park is hemmed up against the rail, and some unnamed cowgirl takes the early lead, so fast her hat flies off.

The horses are gone less than a second before they reappear in the distance, rounding the corner, and we realize that most of the race has been run off-camera, yet another casualty of the filmmaker's inability to move his machine. But things have remained much as they were throughout the backstretch—Miss Lucille looks confident in her slight lead, though Miss Iva has managed to stake her claim on the inside rail, forcing her rivals out into the center of the track. A white pony (riderless) got loose to join the race, and surprisingly, he is not dead last. In fact, he gallops close behind Miss Iva Park's horse, who veers even closer to the rail, pitching his unprepared rider over his left shoulder as his knees crash into the fence. Miss Iva Park's skull breaks her fall at the exact second that Miss Lucille crosses the finish line.

We can only imagine how the filmmaker's pulse thundered at the promise of authentic, unstaged human drama—how he spun the camera toward the two white-clad fellows in charge of the stretcher, and told them to hold a second, so he could make certain that the shot of them rushing to the fallen cowgirl's aid was in perfect focus.

The stretcher-bearers' grins are grim. Neither man has ever been in a movie before, or even seen a camera, so that's exciting; but Miss Iva Park might die, so they must hurry past, trotting diagonally across the track toward the accident. A few seconds later than one would like, a doctor carrying a briefcase and a nurse in a starched pinafore chase after the stretcher. The doctor runs faster than the nurse, who takes so long to reach the patient that the filmmaker lost patience and trimmed a length of frames, resulting in her ghostly teleportation across the screen. When she rematerializes, she stoops to retrieve Miss Iva Park's hat, then shades the patient's face with it, hustling to keep pace with the stretcher as the little convoy crosses the track. As they draw into focus, we see the gray crosses on the rescuers' sleeves and are reassured.

Although dazed, Miss Iva Park remembers to turn toward the camera as she is borne past. Sweaty curls cling to her forehead, and she keeps her leather-gloved hands folded over her chest, but she doesn't die in this movie.

**Miss Lucille Mulhall introducing
Tiny Mite, the smallest bucking
Horse in the world.
This pony cannot be ridden.**

All of the spectators in this movie are on horseback, ranged behind a low split-rail fence, a detail which suggests that the event documented was held for the private amusement of the cowboys and the camera, and not as an official act in C.L. Harris's "Passing of the West" rodeo gala.

Three men in broad Stetsons form a triangle around Miss Lucille's "Tiny Mite" while a clown with smeared makeup holds either side of the miniature bronco's halter. The clown is trying to stop Tiny Mite from rearing, but the pony is already pogoing backwards, hooves slashing at a cowboy with the number 52 pinned to his back. Mr. 52 pulls the lead rope taut, dragging Tiny Mite down, and the clown seizes his chance to swing his leg over. We are watching a child straddle a dog. He gets his knee over the little horse's neck, then slides sideways, clinging to Tiny Mite's belly like a tick until he's thrashed off and under.

What follows is a series of jump cuts that render Tiny Mite's war with the cowboys as an epic montage, escalating in violence over an undisclosed period of time. Whether or not Tiny Mite enjoys this ordeal is unclear. His ears flick like switchblades. We watch him roll onto his back, bucking wildly, then whirl out wide as a kite, snapping 52's rope taut enough to knock him down. A small spotted dog gets involved, nipping at the pony's heels. Twice it enters the danger zone beneath Tiny Mite where each cowboy crashes, shielding their eyes from his hooves. Loose Stetsons spin through the gritty air.

Miss Lucille paces in and out of the frame, supervising. At one point she approaches 52, raising her left hand as if to calm the situation, or protest about the treatment of her animal. But beyond this gesture she does not interfere, even when a man six times the pony's size kneels full on his neck, pinning him to the ground.

We recall that Miss Lucille's heart is rawhide, cured in salt. It will quit on her in 1940, behind the wheel of a red Stutz Super Bearcat purchased by her second ex-husband. She gets t-boned in an intersection mere miles away from the family seat in Mulhall, Oklahoma, about a decade after this camera ceases cranking.

We do not rewind, but let the reel spin out until it flaps in the projector, a loose wing.

MIDWEST UTILITOR BREAKDOWN

Uncle Lad found Blackie grazing along the main road between here and Moberly. No bridle, no harness—just a big black horse with good young teeth who broke loose from someone, or maybe raced the train and lost. Mama says Lad undid his own belt, slung it around Blackie's neck, and tamed him with whispers. But it's hard to know what to believe about Uncle Lad anymore. Since we put in the Midwest Utilitor, only the nicest things are said, in Bible voices.

Mornings, Uncle Lad used to gallop Blackie along the fence line, and I'd use my finger to follow the dark dot that was them across my windowpane, their shared shadow short in the tall grass. A spit of bubbles in the glass sliced them clean in two, so for a second Blackie looked like both halves of a horse costume, and Uncle Lad was the headless horseman. But they always came out right together on the other side, hey presto!

Back then we only had about twenty head of hogs, fat snorting porkers who only stood to eat, their swollen stomachs slung so low they scraped the barn floor. There were chickens, too, and of course the horses had to be fed and watered before Pop needed them for the plow. These chores were mine. Most mornings I got along pretty well, lugging buckets of cold well water that splashed my knees, slinging grain sacks over my shoulder like some girl-shaped mule. Old Jack was good when I fed him—he'd wait in the corner of his stall while I filled his manger and come snuffling forward after I left. But oh, that Blackie was a devil. He had teeth like roofing nails, and a nasty trick of swinging his rump around to pin me to the wall before I could dump his grain. Pop'd be out oiling the old drag harrow, I'd scream, and then Mama would come running barefoot, hollering how a girl of ten was far too young to be left alone with that goddamned animal, until Uncle Lad hooked his thumbs under my armpits and pulled me out from under Blackie, laughing his hoarse laugh like I wasn't bawling my eyes out.

This happened often enough that even Uncle Lad had to admit that Blackie wasn't quite right in the head. An orphan foal, he guessed, pulled hind-first out of his mama to be bottle-fed in some petticoated lady's drawing room until every lick of sense was petted and cosseted out of his thick black skull. Then, when he got too big to keep, he probably got packed off to some sale barn without any consideration for his particular circumstances, like he was just some machine, which is no way to handle an animal. You put good in, you get good out. This, said Uncle Lad proudly, is why your Pop can't do nothing with him.

That much was true. Sometimes Pop would be riding behind the plow and Blackie would spook right out of harness, snapping the traces. Sometimes he kicked out with both back legs, and Pop had to jump clear off the plow so his ribcage wouldn't get smashed like a cider barrel. Then there was always a big fuss, and we'd waste a day chasing Blackie and Old Jack through the woods, getting cut up on briars. The south fields had to get plowed, though, and we only had our horses to do it, unless we could trade for better. Pop managed to convince some of the neighbor men to come take a look, but they all checked Old Jack's teeth, clucked their tongues, had a go-round chasing Blackie with a rope, and ended up shaking their heads at us, like Pop was some big cheat. When you have a bad horse, Pop said, word travels like water. By summer, no one even came to look anymore. So it was a real surprise when the engine man's truck came grinding up our access road, chrome fender scattering chickens as it came.

Mama was dishing up bacon hash, Uncle Lad and Pop were on their second cups of coffee, and I was dipping toast in yolk when we saw the big white van lumbering past the barn. There was a bit of a commotion, what with Mama spilling coffee and the yard dogs barking and Lad banging out the screen door after them. But Pop just set his mug down and tugged his napkin off his neck.

"That'll be the man from the engine company," he said to me, since Uncle Lad and Mama were already in the front yard, collaring the yard dogs as they twisted and lurched at the van. A thin red coat of clay from our access road clung to the gleaming white hood. I felt like I should spit-shine it clean before our guest got out and saw it. I could see him sitting in the cab shuffling papers around, like he couldn't see us stood there waiting on him.

Mama thought maybe he was afraid of the dogs, so she thrust the two half-grown pups she was holding at me. Then Uncle Lad shooed me into the barn, so it ended up that I didn't get a good look at the engine man till he was sitting at our breakfast table, eating bread slicked orange with Mama's blue ribbon persimmon jam. That stuff made my teeth pucker, but somehow our guest smiled as he chewed. He wore a gray worsted suit, like the men in Mama's *Photoplay*, and I caught a whiff of talcum powder whenever he moved. Mama shooed me to the stool by the dry-sink with a pay-attention look. Her people were city folks, so she thought anything from there was cultural, even a salesman with lean earthworm fingers.

"Well, first of all, thank you for sending for a free demonstration, and for your hospitality," he was saying. "I'm here to show you how automating your farm with the Midwest Utilitor cultivator will reduce your expenses, improve your yields, and give you more time to relax—all at a price you can afford. You see, the Midwest Utilitor is what we call a 'vest pocket tractor,' on account of its compact size and affordability."

"Is that right," said Pop, squinting at the brochures the engine man handed him. His greasy thumbs smeared the glossy paper.

"It's guaranteed dependable power, sir. Now, be honest with me— how many horses do you keep on your property?"

"Just two," said Pop. "But one's old, he don't work."

"But you still feed him, don't you, sir? You put in your time and money, day after day, and for what? The truth is, you're really *working for horses*. You keep horses to raise corn—and raise corn to feed horses—all so you can raise more corn for more horses. What's the *use*? Use your brain and save your back, that's what I say. Why, just one gasoline-powered, water-cooled Midwest Utilitor provides the pulling power of four strong horses for only five cents an hour. Compare that to the cost per head of keeping horses fed and shod, not to mention the hassle and worry, and you'll see sense: horse farming is *wrong*. Park your Utilitor in the barn and forget about it until you need it. It works for you, not the other way around."

The dusty windowpane behind the engine man framed Uncle Lad out in the sideyard, wrestling rusty bundles of chicken wire. I was supposed to be there, helping him fix the fence. But then the engine man thumped his fist on the table, and I forgot all about it again. "And best of all, the Utilitor is multipurpose," he went on. "As a tractor it plows, harrows, cultivates, mows, and pulls small loads; as a stationary engine it saws wood, pumps water, and even churns butter, with the right attachment. But you've looked over the literature already, and I'm done bending your ear. It's high time you saw the genuine article in action."

We trooped out into the sunshine, our guest jingling keys as he jogged toward his vehicle. It was funny, seeing a man dressed so nice hurry like that, kicking red dust up over his shiny shoes. We stood by the barn. The engine man opened the back of his truck. Then we heard a hollow cough, followed by a metallic squeal, and finally a futt-futt-futting rhythm propelled the Midwest Utilitor down the tailgate and into the dust, slowly, slowly, its own small parade.

The Utilitor's engine housing gleamed green as its thick wheels obediently carved a circle in the scrub-grass. The wide tire-treads stamped the earth into uniform squares, its tiny chimney coughing puffs of steam. And behind it all stood the mighty engine-man, steady hands clutching black vinyl handles, grinning teeth vibrating as he guided his mechanical mount to a graceful halt. He descended casually, as if this was the most natural thing in the world for a man, to magic metal to life. It was the first time I remember wanting anything, I mean real wanting, not the usual stabbing pang I get for sugar or magazines, gone as soon as the thing is safe in my hands.

"This model includes the plow attachment!" he shouted over the din. In the absence of a human driver, the tractor futt-futted obediently in its prescribed orbit, awaiting further instruction. It wasn't like Pop's truck, which needed a human foot on the pedal. It went on its own steam, like something deep in its metal chest was urging it on, something, it seemed, that even a girl of ten and three-quarters could command.

This is what I see in the Kodak the engine man took of us, proudly arranged around our brand-new "wheel-horse." Pop has the pinched, thoughtful look he always gets after spending money, even on an installment plan. Mama is only half-there, overexposed in a shaft of light, the twins already brewing in her stomach. I am towheaded in calico, leaning on the Utilitor's sunbaked hood. It was so hot the metal burnt my elbow, but I wasn't moving for anything, I was just that proud.

The change the Utilitor wrought was instantaneous and revolutionary, and all the other big words of progress from the brochures tacked to my bedroom wall. I still had to feed each morning, but I could take my sweet time, since Pop didn't need Blackie and Old Jack anymore. He whiled away the hour he used to spend grooming and harnessing them with an after-breakfast pipe and extra coffee. Then we'd swing wide the barn doors, and our Utilitor would futt-futt-futt through the fields, dragging our plow through the furrows, reliably guided by Uncle Lad.

It was the real handyman around the house or barn, just like the engine man said. The Utilitor plowed slower than the horses, but it didn't bolt or spook, so every row it wrote in the warm earth was straight and true. It couldn't go lame, or kick, or yank the reins out of your hands. So after a while Mama saw no harm in letting me drive it a little, so long as I wore a pair of Uncle Lad's overalls with the ankles tucked into gumboots, and a moth-eaten straw boater against the sun. I started in her kitchen garden. I loved the crunch the big front wheels made as they smashed moldering watermelons, and the way the plow I pulled worked dry tomato stems back into the hungry dirt. To turn, I had to lean hard into the end of each row and brace myself against the handles, a maneuver that made the Utilitor groan and shake in the most thrilling way, like it might flip over at any second—but each time I made it, closing off the row with a neat letter C. Of course Uncle Lad and Pop said it was bad, a girl driving a tractor. But Mama was proud, handing me cold Mason jars of tea when I futt-futted past her clothesline. The Utilitor wasn't fast, but it was still exciting to float along behind it, the juddering motor raising gooseflesh as it shook the metal plate I stood on, then my boots, then all of me, right up to my teeth.

It was around this same time that good Old Jack up and died. I found him beside the water trough, flies lining his dull brown eyes, tongue coated with dust. Blackie was grazing down over the hill. He didn't even care that Old Jack was a goner. That's another thing I don't like about horses, the easy way they abandon the weak and the dead. I ran to get Pop. I knew he'd want to get Old Jack underground before the coyotes got wind of him, but it wasn't a one-man job, like burying a possum or a dog. Mama gathered up all our shovels, even the outhouse one, and the whole family started jumping on their blades with both feet, dredging up thick red hunks of clay.

I wasn't heavy enough to jump on shovels, but with all of us digging to China, it wasn't long before Uncle Lad was standing at the bottom of a pit six feet deep. It was Pop who decided that we'd use the Utilitor to pull Old Jack down into it. Use your brain and save your back, he said. He got a length of chain from the barn and wound it around Old Jack's ankles while Uncle Lad maneuvered the Utilitor into position on the other side of the hole, futt-futt-futt. Once Pop had Old Jack hog-tied, he threw the loose end of the chain over to Uncle Lad, who hooked it to the Utilitor's hitch, then scrambled back onto the machine to drive it forward. Pop reckoned that he'd only need to pull the body a few feet to get it to fall into the grave, then I'd climb in to undo the chain, and we'd get the hole filled before suppertime.

There was a spurt of smoke as the Midwest Utilitor got going, its wheels spinning in the hardscrabble, Uncle Lad leaning forward for traction. I'd seen it pull the plow, the harrow, even a nasty root wad that was stuck in the creek, but I guess Old Jack weighed more. His knobby knees stretched to their full length as the Utilitor tugged them toward the hole, loose gray skin slipping over bone. I thought they'd tear in half before Uncle Lad ever moved that horse. But somehow he managed to inch Old Jack closer and closer, until the horse's swollen belly teetered on one edge of the grave, and Uncle Lad and the Utilitor huffed and spluttered on the other, the short chain drawn taut between them.

Then he gave it the gas.

The rest comes back to me in snapshots, like I wasn't even there, like the whole horrible scene was documented for someone to pore over in their parlor, cluck sympathetically, and feel some strange relief that it didn't happen to their family. Mama screaming, her mouth a wide gray O. The dull moan of failing iron. The sweet reek of gasoline. Old Jack's pink tongue clenched between yellow teeth. And Uncle Lad sandwiched between horse and tractor, his spine twisted against the side of the hole.

We buried them both that day, after the neighbor men pulled the Utilitor out.

BASED ON A
TRUE STORY

I. TRAVOLTA, BORED

If these are the days of miracle and wonder, then John Travolta's performance in *The Boy in the Plastic Bubble* (1976) is a long-distance call. Just 22, Travolta sports the luxurious black bouffant of our cultural memory. He wears gym shorts, yellow with white piping, and a powder blue tee chosen to echo his glacial eyes. A plaid tam o'shanter with a pompon completes the groovy wardrobe of Tod Lubitch, titular Boy, who remains with-it despite the confines of his plastic prison.

Nearby, industrial fans whir, keeping the ersatz Bubble in a state of constant inflation. Randal Kleiser, the director of this ABC Friday Night Movie, loves to remind John Travolta that the shooting set is an exact replica of the state-of-the-art units inhabited by the real Bubble Boys. There are two of them out there, living aquarium lives.

The most famous of the pair, David Vetter IV, has severe combined immunodeficiency disorder. The same genetic anomaly killed his brother, David III, just eight weeks before David IV's conception. But the bereft Vetters were determined to have a son. Their grieving pediatricians supported their decision, as SCID research at Texas Children's Hospital would be accelerated with a live subject to study, a boy kept safe in an incubator from the moment of birth, hypoallergenic, immaculate. A practicing Catholic, Mrs. Vetter placed her faith in medicine. David Vetter IV was just five when *The Boy in the Plastic Bubble* (1976) was filmed, but Tod Lubitch's origin story follows Vetter's to the letter.

The movie's other source, Maryland's Ted DeVita, is fourteen during production, much closer to Tod Lubitch in age. Unlike Vetter, Ted was normal and healthy until age nine, when he broke out in purple splotches at the dinner table. His father, an oncologist at the National Institute of Health, diagnosed him with aplastic anemia on the spot. Since that awful evening, Ted has lived in a laminar airflow room in a NIH ward, fiddling with his ham radio and seeing his family often. By all accounts, Ted is psychologically normal; a smart, affable guy who practices magic tricks on his nurses, plays electric guitar, and enjoys *Star Trek*.

Neither the DeVitas nor the Vetters agreed to *The Boy in The Plastic Bubble*, calling it cheap exploitation. The families didn't want their sons involved in "disease of the week" sensationalism. But the film can receive billing as a "fact-based teleplay," in part because between takes, John Travolta reads magazine articles on Vetter and DeVita, meditating on their shared plight. The boys can only be touched through black vinyl sleeves, and everything they consume, even pills, must first be decontaminated with ethylene oxide gas. Unsmiling, David and Ted stare up at John Travolta through *Newsweek* spreads, the boys' sterile glares reflected in the fisheye lenses the photographer chose to accentuate their isolation.

At 22, John Travolta is already a method actor. He leans back in his canvas chair, shuts those malamute eyes, and tries to picture all the negative energies that must cling to the real Bubble Boys' cavefish skin. Travolta wonders whether negativity can permeate space-age polymers, diffuse and invisible, then suppresses a shudder—really getting into character.

On set, director Randal Kleiser has reinforced the symbolism of Tod Lubitch's plight with a pet "hypoallergenic" white mouse, really a pet shop feeder rescued by the prop guy. John Travolta named the mouse Cagney, after the gangster actor. (*Cagney & Lacey* wouldn't premiere until 1981.) Travolta's intent here is unknown, but the name does emphasize Tod Lubitch's reliance on old movie reruns for acculturation to the outside world, while simultaneously reinforcing his sublimated man-child rage. Cagney the mouse is present throughout the film, his orange Habitrail snaking through Tod's vinyl warren, a cage within a cage.

Within a cage, if we count the Malibu Lake, California home rented for the shoot. Production is on-location so Tod Lubitch can use the second-floor window to spy on Gina, the pretty neighbor who smokes dope on the lakeside patio below. The Bubble Boy owns an expensive set of binoculars, which means at some point his parents bought and sterilized and gave them to him, actively encouraging his peeping Tomhood. Gina is tanned and nubile. She also owns a horse.

For a "fact-based teleplay" about a housebound teenager, there are a surprising number of exterior scenes in *The Boy in the Plastic Bubble*. These include a fireworks display at the beach, a midday smoking circle on the high school's fifty-yard line, and multiple outdoor sequences involving Gina's horse, who is a metaphor.

To shoot these, John Travolta is loaded into a smaller, portable Bubble and wheeled out on a gurney, or zipped into a quilted orange spacesuit, complete with tentacular ventilation tubes. Each time he dons the spacesuit, which looks like a full-body oven mitt, John Travolta doubts whether he should be starring in this movie.

His agent swears the ABC Friday Night Movie is a prestige slot. But Travolta is wary of being typecast as a TV actor, like *The Brady Bunch's* Robert Reed, who is coincidentally playing the Bubble Boy's dad. Of course, *Welcome Back, Kotter's* a runaway hit, and John Travolta likes seeing himself on the cover of *Tiger Beat* and *Dynamite*, pink hearts of teen lust bubbling around his fresh household name. But he wants to be taken seriously, too. Each role will shape how we see him, what's expected from a John Travolta picture. He explained this to his agent, who countered that the Bubble is a classic Hitchcockian environmental constraint, like the apartment set in *Rope* or the lifeboat in *Lifeboat*—a real chance to flex his dramatic chops.

Eager to market himself as an actor who can dance, John Travolta only agreed to *The Boy in the Plastic Bubble* after his agent convinced Randal Kleiser to add a short scene to the film. In it, Travolta discos before a pink and orange lightboard, installed to make the Bubble read more futuristic onscreen. Despite the limited space available to boogie, Tod Lubitch is a surprisingly confident dancer, light on his stocking feet.

Nearby, Cagney spins in his wheel, achieving parabolic flight.

II. THE MONSTER NEXT DOOR

Gina Biggs, teen object of the Bubble Boy's binocular lust, is played by an up-and-comer named Glynnis O'Connor. Gina is clearly Tod's love interest, because she is the only named woman in the movie other than Tod's mom.

Our germ-crossed lovers meet as toddlers: Gina played by twin girls, Tod by an eerily Travoltaic infant who was told the mobile containment unit was a playhouse, then given unlimited Coca-Cola. Little Toddy flings himself at Diana Hyland through the plastic, obliviously enacting both the boy's early innocence of his condition and John Travolta's quasi-Oedipal desires for Hyland, who, when they're not in character as mother and son, seems kind of into him, sidling up behind his chair.

In this scene the Lubitches are wheeling toddler Tod's portable Bubble up their suburban sidewalk. Fed up with splitting family life between home and hospital, the young Lubitches are determined to care for Toddy on their own terms, though neither has any medical training whatsoever. Later this evening, Tod will almost choke on the button eye of his hypoallergenic teddy as his parents attempt passionate our-son's-home-from-the-hospital sex in the next room.

Soon reporters and paparazzi mob the struggling couple, shoving microphones at Robert Reed's formidable mustache. "My son's not a FREAK!" he barks as the luminous Diana Hyland struggles to hoist her son's life-support system over the concrete stoop alone. Caffeinated, baby Tod claws at his vinyl capsule.

Meanwhile, fiendish girl-next-door Gina presses her chubby cheeks against the Bubble, screeching, "I'm a monster! I'm a monster! I'm a monster!" at the giggling boy inside. It is unclear if Gina is referring to Tod or herself.

This ambiguity is reinforced in the very next scene, where Gina has aged into Glynnis O'Connor, acquiring the wild eyes of a Manson sister and Breck commercial hair. Perpetually attended by a pair of surfer guys, teen Gina's hobbies include horseback riding, smoking, and mocking the sad, sad life of the neighbor boy, who has remained uncontaminated long enough to grow into John Travolta. Gina tells the surfers she sees Tod once a year at his birthday party, where she has always been the only guest. His parents tape multicolored balloons and streamers onto the Bubble, her folks buy a present for her to give him, and there's sterilized cake.

Naturally, Gina's acquaintance with the local kid shut-in leads her friends to bet she can't make Tod leave his house for the Fourth of July beach shindig. Because she takes dares, Gina visits Tod's house to invite him. John Travolta bounces, puppylike, at the reverse vacuumed entrance to the Bubble. Gina stands tantalizingly out of reach, beyond the masking tape demarcating the sterile zone, close enough for him to smell the powdery chemistry of her Love's Baby Soft.

"You think I'm beautiful, don't you?" asks Gina, eyes flaring. "So do I."

The camera lingers on John Travolta's stocking feet. He is literally toeing the taped line, stark yellow against the beige carpet.

"Of course I'll come to the party," Tod gushes, trying and failing to seem cool, which in 1976 was a genuine challenge for John Travolta.

III. BEACH BUBBLE BINGO

After a commercial break, Tod's parents have wheeled him to the beach for the Fourth of July bonfire. If real, this outing would be prohibitively risky for an immunocompromised person, as any errant spark from the bonfire might ignite the oxygen-rich unit, causing medical inferno. But Randal Kleiser wants a horse to symbolize freedom in this movie, so here we are.

"Happy Fourth of July, son!" shouts Robert Reed, mustache dominating the frame as he gazes down at Tod, subjective camera.

"What do you think of my horse?" asks Glynnis-as-Gina, cantering the animal over to the Bubble, trying to taunt Tod with her sexy autonomy. Oblivious, John Travolta sits cross-legged and grins inside the capsule, enjoying the beach party music. He is astonishingly pale—"a real tuna fish," as he'll later declare.

"Oh, I *love* him," gushes John Travolta, awestruck by Gina's horse and bikini. He figures Tod's never seen either phenomenon up close, let alone the ocean beyond her, so he grabs his knees, rocking back and forth. "I watch you feed him every morning! And I love to watch you ride him!"

"Do you always talk like that?" asks Gina, annoyed. "I love this, I love that..."

"But I do!" yelps John Travolta. "I really do!"

Astride her horse, Gina towers over Tod. It shifts beneath her, ears flattened, teeth bared. It hates the Bubble.

"Yeah, but I mean you shouldn't tell people. They'll think you're dumb."

John Travolta frowns.

"So you like my horse, huh?" asks Gina, tossing the line away as she canters into the darkness. "Maybe I'll let you ride him when you get out."

Inside his incubator, John Travolta rocks compulsively, somehow embodying both Tod's stunted lust and childlike longing to go horseback riding. Later, Gina returns on foot, and they hold hands through Tod's black neoprene access glove. There are fireworks when they touch because it is the Fourth of July. Gina earns two whole dollars from the kids she's really there to hang out with. She collects the cash in front of Tod as violent piano arpeggios accent his inner turmoil.

Randal Kleiser directed John Travolta to play this scene as though he has no grip on rational human emotions. Therefore, Tod reacts to Gina's betrayal with complete meltdown, slapping and kicking the portable Bubble's walls and padded liner. He looks like he's having a seizure. Frantic, Robert Reed flies to his side, grabbing at the Bubble's vacuum tubing, checking dials. Meanwhile, Diana Hyland, who will win the Primetime Emmy for Outstanding Performance by a Supporting Actress in a Comedy or Drama Special for her role as Tod's mom, shrieks the teen's childhood nickname again and again in front of the startled partygoers.

"What's wrong, Toddy? Toddy, honey! Toddy! What's wrong?"

IV. BUZZ ALDRIN AS HIMSELF

The Boy in the Plastic Bubble is an ABC Friday Night Movie. In 1976, this means it's up against the *Sonny & Cher Show*, the CBS Friday Night Movie, and later that evening, *Serpico*. Most of Travolta's usual demographic discos on Friday nights, so halfway through principal photography, ABC decided a celebrity cameo could seal the deal with the older crowd, who also need to see advertisements for Winston-Salems and McDonald's.

When pressed for a name, director Randal Kleiser saw poetry in the parallels between the Apollo astronauts' 1969 voyage in the cramped lunar module and Tod's lifelong encapsulation. Neil Armstrong was busy, so they got Buzz Aldrin. Still, because his cameo was not part of the original shooting script, there is a stilted randomness to the astronaut's appearance in the film's final cut.

It goes like this: after the Fourth of July beach party, Tod demands to be sent back to the safety of the hospital, where his parents can't embarrass him in front of girls. He is assigned a laminar airflow room adjacent to a temporarily immunocompromised teen named Roy (John Friedrich). Wearing matching short-shorts on either side of a Plexiglas barrier, the boys in their Bubbles ride exercise bikes and discuss masturbation.

"I *want* the germs!" shrieks Roy, unhinged mouthpiece of Tod's shadow-self. "I want to make it with *everything that moves!*"

Both laugh, pedaling furiously. It is Roy's first and last appearance in this movie.

Meanwhile, Gina and one of her surfer friends neck on a pea-green Naugahyde couch in her parents' basement, cuddled amid granny afghans and the cold glow of the local news. The petting's getting heavy when Gina is distracted.

"Elsewhere in the news, astronaut Buzz Aldrin visits young Tod Lubitch, the boy who has grown up inside a plastic bubble."

"That's Tod!" gasps Gina, pushing her date away to grab the television remote, which in 1976 is still an indicator of her family's high economic status. She stabs at the volume button, leaning toward the screen. "I want to see this, hold on. He's coming home next week."

"So what?" snarls the surfer.

Gina's T.V. dominates the frame, its black plastic edges and metallic knobs making sure we know what we're about to see is also being broadcast within the diegetic world of the film. This is director Randal Kleiser's artful attempt to insert a Buzz Aldrin guest spot into a scene that also advances the plot. We are meant to read Gina's mid-clinch fascination with Tod's random astronaut meet-and-greet as a mark of her growing romantic interest. This will distract from the fact that Buzz Aldrin is a cheap ratings grab.

Buzz Aldrin reaches through a black vinyl sleeve to shake Tod's hand. The camera draws back from this symbolic gesture to frame the two of them in a wider shot, presenting their meeting with staged cinematography at odds with the usual *mise-en-scène* of nightly news reportage.

"You're Buzz Aldrin, aren't you?" asks John Travolta. "The man who walked on the moon," he adds, in case younger viewers haven't caught on.

Starstruck, he flops back onto his hospital bed. "Oh, I don't believe this!"

But it's Buzz Aldrin, all right. In close-up, just one sheet of plastic separates his famous face from the lens. To physically shoot this footage, the news camera would have had to be standing inside the Bubble with Tod, ruining his sterile environment. It is one of several such gaffes in the movie.

"I've been looking forward to meeting you, Tod," says Buzz Aldrin, wooden, like he thinks this is a play. "I hear you have the record for the longest time in a command module."

"Yeah, I guess so!" says John Travolta, drying his palms on the sides of his yellow shorts.

"I got a little something for you, too," says Buzz Aldrin. The camera cuts to a black-and-white signed photograph of Aldrin himself in full moonwalk gear (sterile?), which he shoves into the Bubble through a plastic chute.

"To Tod, champion spaceman on Earth," breathes John Travolta, hugging the picture. "Thank you. Hey, you spent some time in one of these things, didn't you? Right after the moon flight."

"Something very much like it, Tod," replies Buzz Aldrin. "We were in germ-controlled quarters for several weeks."

"Well, what was it like for you?" asks John Travolta.

"The thing I remember most was the loss of freedom," says Buzz Aldrin, struggling to find pathos in the line. "You know, it felt like being in a fishbowl."

John Travolta looks glum. "Yeah, I know what you mean."

"Tod Lubitch, the boy who will spend the rest of his life in a plastic bubble," interrupts the demulcent anchorwoman.

Cut back to Gina and the annoyed surfer on her basement couch. Gina, mesmerized by Tod's media triumph, is clutching her hands to her mouth like a squirrel. Turned on by her vulnerability, Gina's date reaches for her, but she sidles away, saying her parents will be home soon, he's got to go.

"What is it with you and that freak?" growls the surfer, denied.

"He's my next-door neighbor," protests Gina. "We grew up together! Is anything wrong with that? Don't call him a *freak*!"

V. HORSE AS SYMBOL

Gina's unnamed horse is one of many figurative liberties taken by *The Boy in the Plastic Bubble*, which like all motion pictures in the "disease of the week" genre, is more invested in tearjerking melodrama than strict adherence to medical truth. In the film, the horse's sensual or physical nature, embodied by the feminine Gina, is placed in direct opposition to the spiritual and mental nature of man, represented by Tod and his caged counterpart, Cagney the hypoallergenic mouse.

In this sense, *The Boy in the Plastic Bubble* is clumsily Jungian.

The horse itself was hired from an animal talent firm popular among Western directors during the 1970s. There are two, actually— one animal docile enough to be ridden by Glynnis O'Connor, novice equestrienne, and a second, more spirited individual, who is used for stunt work. When he first read the script, director Randal Kleiser envisioned Gina's horse as a palomino—a golden bolt, superheroic and soaring. "Like Trigger," he told his assistants. "Get me a Trigger."

The horses that play Gina's are plain chestnuts, the kind usually cast as sidekicks' mounts and background scenery. Randal Kleiser was disappointed at first, then decided that a brown horse, run-of-the-mill as it is, might visually reinforce Tod's longing for normalcy. Ridden by the proverbial girl-next-door, the animal becomes a clear metaphor for what he's missing.

These particular horses are used to galloping through gunfire and leaping over ravines, so they spook at the sterile hiss of the portable Bubble, having never encountered state-of-the-art medical equipment in the cinematic West. Stunt-Gina is a strong rider, but either horse freezes, snorting, whenever she reins it within six feet of the Bubble. The animals fear John Travolta moving around behind the clear plastic, unable to smell him through the vinyl tang of his billowy cocoon.

Equine actors, like children, can only work a few hours per day. If it takes two hours to get them to perform a behavior, that's valuable time John Travolta and Glynnis O'Connor spend waiting in their trailers, getting paid not to make this movie. Concerned, ABC sends executives to the set to ask if a cheaper, more tractable animal might symbolize Tod's desire for freedom and transcendence and Gina—an escape-prone parakeet, perhaps, or a box of butterflies. But Randal Kleiser is unwilling to budge on his artistic choices. He believes there's something primal about a woman on a horse.

So, in the early third act sequence that forms *The Boy in the Plastic Bubble*'s emotional climax, we are asked to accept that during the commercial break, Tod Lubitch convinced his parents to vacation in Hawaii, exposing their fragile son to the twin threats of inadequate sterilization and peer pressure. As soon as Robert Reed and Diana Hyland drive away, the camera cuts to Gina galumphing up to Tod's room, excited to show off her report card: straight As. For weeks, lovestruck Tod has been transmitting correct answers to Gina (and the rest of the class) via closed-circuit television while Mr. Brister's back is turned. When she presses her good grades against the plastic, John Travolta cracks his most beatific grin.

"That's great, Gina," he sighs.

Gina says they should celebrate. She says they can do anything he wants. Tod asks if he can watch her go horseback riding, because he's emotionally twelve. Tod's skeptical nurse, Rachel, is soon drafted to help Gina drag his porta-Bubble into the backyard, using an extension cord to keep his life-support plugged into the house. Once they're out there, John Travolta informs Nurse Rachel she can go inside now, then joins Gina in giggling about his casual rudeness to the help.

"Gina, ride for me, okay?"

Glynnis O'Connor turns to mount her horse, which is already saddled and bridled because no one wants to see a grooming montage.

"Gina! Go around that tree, jump over the canoe, then come back to me as fast as you can!" hollers John Travolta.

Cut to a long shot of Stunt-Gina astride the friskier chestnut, cantering toward the tree. She performs the requested equestrian feats as we crosscut between her riding and reaction shots of a gleeful Travolta, who rocks back and forth inside his porta-Bubble, hugging himself. Buttery trumpets sound.

"Gina! You move so fast! What does it feel like to move that fast?"

"It feels like flying," sighs Gina, giddy with symbolism.

"Gina, ride around me in a circle, as close as you can!"

"But what about the cord?" she protests.

"What about the cord? You just jumped over a canoe, you can jump over that stupid cord!"

"What about your nurse?"

"Oh, this is the time of day when she drinks sherry," says John Travolta. "She just sits there and watches the plug, and makes sure it doesn't come out, and gets pleasantly bombed."

If what Tod's saying is true, Nurse Rachel endangers his life on a daily basis. Gina seems to find this hilarious.

"Come on, Gina, do it."

"Okay," agrees Glynnis O'Connor, still laughing.

The camera cuts to a long shot as Stunt-Gina clucks her horse into action, riding in a tight circle around and around the mysteriously cordless porta-Bubble. Inside, John Travolta spins on his haunches, crying "Faster, Gina! Faster!"

"Now jump over me, Gina!"

"*No way*, Tod," laughs Glynnis O'Connor, sawing the bit in her horse's mouth.

"Gina, you jumped over the canoe! I've seen you jump twice this high!"

"What if I miss?"

"Gina, you won't miss! I know you, you're too talented to miss!" shouts Tod, earnest despite overwhelming evidence that Gina's real talent is emotional manipulation.

"Tod, you are really a weird kid, you know that?" says Glynnis O'Connor. Something about the way she delivers the line unconsciously normalizes the absolutely insane thing that's about to happen in this movie.

"Yeah, I know it, just do it, Gina, okay?"

"Okay," she relents.

As Stunt-Gina circles her horse behind some pines, picking up a trot, we cut to the black plug in the dining room outlet. The camera pulls back to reveal Nurse Rachel sitting in the Lubitches' dining room, sherry glass in hand. Meanwhile, back inside the Bubble, John Travolta's stunt double assumes a cheesecake pose, elbow propping his fluffy black wig. Rapid crosscuts between galloping Stunt-Gina, panicked Nurse Rachel, and a wonderstruck close up of John Travolta build momentum as the horse bears down on the Bubble, to a fanfare of trilling strings.

"Dear Lord!" gasps Nurse Rachel, on cue.

The camera follows the horse in slow-mo. This is the only shot in the film where this effect is used. It took seven takes for Stunt-Gina to launch the horse over Stunt-Tod, who is seen only from behind. On screen, Gina's golden tresses fly as the horse sails over the medical obstacle, the arc of his spine kissing the Ektachrome sky, his back an inversion of the background valley. It is the money shot, inspired by a 1930s promotional photograph of a horse leaping over a convertible. Randal Kleiser liked the simplicity of the image: the literality of nature overcoming the machine.

In the take used, the horse's back hooves nick the edge of the Bubble as it landed. This fortuitous mistake was accentuated in post-production by having foley artists punch sheet metal. In the film's final cut, this effect translates into brief viewer panic as we watch the Plexiglas wobble and think for a split-second that Gina's burst Tod's

Bubble, flooding his lungs with germs. But John Travolta looks fine, panting on his vinyl mat like a happy retriever. Exhausted, Glynnis O'Connor dismounts, letting her horse wander away with its bridle on, and sags into the grass beside the isolator unit.

"That was so great!" John Travolta snickers, rolling around on foam padding.

"I was so scared. Were you scared?"

"Not once," says Tod.

Gina doesn't believe him. They breathe heavily on either side of the plastic, exhilarated by risk, teenage and desperate. Gina asks Tod when he's going to get out of that Bubble. Just as he sighs he doesn't know, Gina's blonde basement date from earlier pulls up in a blue convertible, honks, and suddenly she's "gotta split."

"I'll be back later to help you get inside, okay?" Gina tells Tod, even though this is California, so she's basically leaving him in a human oven bag. Her horse is left wandering in Tod's yard with his saddle on, reins dragging in the grass.

"Which one is *he*?" asks Tod, coldly.

Exasperated, Gina explains that the interloper is obviously Tom, because Bruce drives a Chevy, everyone knows that. Moisture condenses inside the Bubble, clouding John Travolta's pout as Gina claims she isn't really *going* with anyone.

Then (she's a monster, she said so) Gina commands Tod to press his mouth against the plastic so she can "kiss" him, right in front of Tom. Afterward, she giggles and runs toward the blue convertible, abandoning John Travolta like a backyard toy.

VII. CHAMPION SPACEMEN ON EARTH

One puzzling bit of apocrypha remains regarding *The Boy in the Plastic Bubble*. Sometime between its initial broadcast on November 1, 1976 and their deaths in 1984 and 1980, aged 12 and 18 respectively, it seems that both David Vetter IV and Ted DeVita were given opportunities to watch the movie.

It remains unclear why the unconnected teams of child psychologists responsible for the emotional hygiene of two immunocompromised boys whose lives were conflated into an escape fantasy starring John Travolta thought either child should be exposed to the finished film. The impulse seems cruel at best.

Like most American children of the late 1970s, David Vetter IV was a big *Star Wars* (1977) fan. Unlike his peers, he got to watch it *daily* on a state-of-the-art TV/VCR combo his nurses kept wheeled up against the plastic. A bright and acquiescent boy who sports C-3PO and *Sesame Street* t-shirts in the photographs, David was aware of the difference between TV and reality, having discussed it at length with his nurse. Still, the sight of John Travolta rocking back and forth in his television Bubble must have been an odd mirror for young David Vetter IV, sitting criss-cross applesauce in footie pajamas on the padded floor of the real thing.

Because he saw the film on tape, long after its initial release, it is plausible that *The Boy in the Plastic Bubble* was shown to David Vetter as a kind of training video-cum-celebrity endorsement for the $50,000 spacesuit NASA gave him in 1977, a year after the film's initial broadcast. Young David's first excursion in the suit was a rare instance of life imitating art, and thus a perfect subject for the ABC evening news. Archival footage shows David at the zoo, playing with a garden hose, and holding his mother's hand as they stride through a parking lot.

At first David liked his spacesuit. But after just a few outings, the boy's fear of contamination took over. He began having nightmares about the microscopic King of Germs, who assaulted the Bubble nightly with his 9,000 wives, puncturing the plastic with fingernails made of butterfly sutures. Soon David refused to slide down the chute that led to his suit, and since no one could touch him, no one could make him. His isolation gave him a weird autonomy. He'd agree to go out, then pee on the floor of his Bubble so his nurses had to focus on emergency sterilization instead of prepping his spacesuit.

One can imagine a well-meaning and frustrated psychiatrist coaxing David to sit down to watch *The Boy in the Plastic Bubble*, fingers crossed that Randal Kleiser's heady cocktail of sexual empowerment and animal metaphors would inspire the stubborn boy to crave the world beyond his Bubble. Accounts of David's actual reaction to the film are scant. It's said he made gagging noises whenever John Travolta and Glynnis O'Connor kissed, and asked repeatedly why Tod had a pet mouse instead of a goldfish bowl perched outside his Bubble. It's said that David cackled during the part where Tod walks right into the isolator wearing his NASA-designed suit without undergoing the six-step decontamination process David knew such a transfer required.

Overall, David seems to have considered the film a comedy, which is how children view most TV, if only to cope. His nurses noted that the movie seemed to give him a sense of mastery over his situation. He was the *real* boy in the Bubble; he alone knew where they'd gotten the details wrong. Unfortunately, the film didn't inspire him to reenter his spacesuit. It did have one lasting effect on David, however—soon after screening the movie, the King of Germs took up horseback riding, acquiring an army of chargers for his pestilent wives.

Though he is the obvious source for Tod's name, Ted DeVita is often overlooked as a major inspiration for John Travolta's performance in *The Boy in the Plastic Bubble*, due to David Vetter's much wider fame. Wary of the press's effect on their son's psyche, the DeVita family granted fewer interviews than the Vetters. In the newspaper photographs that do exist, longhaired Ted DeVita crosses his arms over his sweatshirt or strums his electric guitar. Like David Vetter, Ted owned a NASA suit. Once he wore it to a *Star Trek* convention—a day he cherishes as the first time since his diagnosis he was able to blend in. Family and friends describe Ted as "alternately hostile, angry, and cheery," in other words, a teenager.

Being closer in age to Tod Lubitch than little David, Ted was aware of *The Boy in the Plastic Bubble*'s release as it happened. He'd noticed Travolta on the cover of his sterilized *TV Guide*: he liked Vinnie Barbarino. But the more Ted read about the movie, the angrier he got. By the night of the broadcast, he was convinced someone in the hospital had leaked information to the producers—a nurse, a NASA rep, maybe even his dad. The violation made him paranoid. Ted refused to see the movie, saying, "I have to live it, why should I watch it?"

Ted's parents joined his boycott, but his younger sister has written about watching the original broadcast of *The Boy in the Plastic Bubble*, alone in her bedroom with the sound turned down. She remembers hating, even then, how the film privileges existence outside the Bubble, implying that the only life her beloved brother could have is a fate worth risking certain death to avoid.

VI. ROLL CREDITS

The finale of *The Boy in the Plastic Bubble* is both ambiguous and bathetic, inviting viewers to read the film as either epiphanic heterosexual liberation or tragic prelude to Tod Lubitch's inevitable off-screen immune collapse.

Banking on the vague pronouncements of his elderly doctor, who has appeared throughout the movie to mention that sometimes people spontaneously generate immune systems, Tod wakes up one random morning, dons an angelic white bell-sleeved shirt and black trousers, takes a deep breath, and steps beyond the womblike confines of his Bubble, aquiver with teenage rebellion.

As soon as John Travolta's feet hit the carpet, the nondiegetic strains of "What Would They Say," the Paul Williams ballad commissioned for the film, swell through the Lubitch house. Tod creeps down the hall to peer at his still slumbering parents in an eerie reversal of their lifelong dynamic. He smiles tenderly, then heads downstairs to pause behind the screen door. Travolta plays the door as a second barrier, spreading his palms across the mesh before he swings the hinges wide, exultant. When he spots Gina grooming her horse, the camera cuts between handheld soft focus from Tod's perspective and a medium reaction shot of John Travolta, the actor's famous grin widening as he sneaks up on Gina—

"Tod!" she cries, shocked to see her heartthrob *en plein air*.

Seizing her, John Travolta rubs his hands all over Glynnis O'Connor's face, because he's never touched another person.

"So much softer than I ever imagined," he murmurs. They kiss, exchanging so many bacteria that, unless Tod's body really has spontaneously generated an immune system, unless that's a thing that can happen—he'll be dead by nightfall. But John Travolta's performance betrays no anxiety or dread. Confidently breaking off the kiss, Tod tosses his head with the authority bucking, risk-taking Travolta bravado that ABC Friday Night Movie and *Welcome Back, Kotter* viewers crave.

"Gina! Take me for a ride!" he chirps, swinging into the saddle behind her. The credits roll over an extreme long shot of the couple galloping down a rural highway, while Paul Williams' reedy baritone croons "Leave us alone, we'd live in the country! Leave us alone, we'd make it just fine! Happy in a one-room shack, and we're not going back, no no…!" The lyrics imply that living in a confined space would be idyllic, if someone else was stuck there, too.

The happy ending of *The Boy in the Plastic Bubble* is both inaccurate and inevitable. It was the only way Randal Kleiser, John Travolta, and America could psychologically process the known, yet unacknowledged truth—that David Vetter and Ted DeVita were never going horseback riding with girls. The real Bubble Boys, stars of *Time* and *Life*, were going to die in isolation, child sacrifices to the space age.

While they lived, every article on Ted or David noted how the world's finest pediatricians had no clue how to fix or free them, how to restore innocent youth to its rightful parade of summer camp, chocolate Quik, and Pong. The public maintained a vague faith that brilliant medical minds were tirelessly titrating blood and marrow, willing dished cells to split. The doctors put the boys in the bubbles in the first place, the act in itself a promise that they'd immediately begin work toward getting them out someday. In reality, neither boy's medical team was close to a cure, though they lived in hope. Like so many human experiments, there was no exit strategy.

But nobody wants to see the ending where Tod Lubitch dies pale and writhing on a gurney, body revolting against the transfusions and transplants meant to prolong his hermetic life. So Hollywood kept the promises science couldn't, giving us a comforting collective memory where medicine is magical and magic is art, and the boy in the Bubble gets to ride off into the sunset, eternally a young John Travolta.

FRED W. LORING AND HIS MULE, "EVIL MERODACH," 48 HOURS BEFORE DEATH

This story is about a man named Frederick Wadsworth Loring. In the stereogram reproduced above (which is the last known image of him) he is shown posing with his saddle mule, "Evil Merodach," somewhere just outside the town of Prescott, Arizona Territory.

It is November 4, 1871. Loring appears youthful and handsome, even in the left frame of the diptych, where the slight shifting necessary to create the illusion of three-dimensional space has smudged deep shadows under his hat and eyes and nose. Canvas tents dominate the background. His shirttail is loose, and his left hand rests just above his hip pocket, which bulges as if concealing whiskey or a gun. These cocksure details remain enough to convince the casual stereogram viewer that Loring is some minor outlaw or train robber, and not a recent graduate of Harvard University, *summa cum laude.*

When this photograph was taken, Frederick Wadsworth Loring

was playing the role of an intrepid freelance journalist on assignment for a New York magazine, following the government-sponsored Wheeler Survey through a part of America that few white men had ever seen. The subject of this stereogram is accustomed to raw oysters, not ground chuck. He misses bathhouses and clean pressed trousers, and no wonder. Just a few months ago, his college friends couldn't contain their laughter when they heard that Loring, the *poet*, was to become a leather-clad king of the wild frontier.

Really, Fred W. Loring went west because his heart was worn raw by love. But this cannot be divined by looking at the picture, which is exactly what he hoped for when he posed for it. He knew that a happy image of himself at home in Arizona would please his widowed father, who had too often heard that his only son and heir was "soft," and needed evidence to the contrary to show his pals. And certainly young Loring enjoyed imagining his own image doubled in a thousand American drawing rooms, sandwiched between buffaloes and ruined pueblos, there to remain until the merry hour when kneeling boys pressed the cold metal stereoscope to their foreheads and crossed their eyes to make "Fred W. Loring and his mule, Evil Merodach" emerge in glorious 3-D.

But beyond these aspirations to front parlor celebrity, Fred W. Loring hoped that his carefree expression would wound Mr. William Wigglesworth Chamberlin to the core as he lounged amid brass and mahogany in a flickering Boston parlor, smoking his postprandial cigar. Perhaps Chamberlin's innocent bride would pass over the stereoscope, in love and wanting to hear him laugh at that funny picture of a man hugging a mule. Then she'd spend the rest of her married life wondering why that silly picture had blanched her new husband's face talcum white.

These unkind thoughts and others thinned Loring's smile as he slung his arm around Evil Merodach's ewe-neck, faced west, and watched the birdie.

***

Prior to the Class of 1870's graduation from Harvard University, Fred W. Loring and Wm. W. Chamberlin were a familiar sight around the Yard. The duo were inseparable due to their mutual passion for Thackeray and a general disdain for anything they deemed "common," a broad list that included baseball, Confederate sympathizers, and suffragettes. Then as now, it wasn't considered strange for young gentlemen at college to form intense attachments to one another, so long as both parties maintained a general chumminess with the other men in their year, and each eventually broke off to marry a respectable lady. Closeted as he'd been at home, Loring found this social milieu both liberating and baffling, particularly when it came to his best friend.

A Boston Brahmin destined for a long career in philanthropy and dinner parties, Chamberlin hurled himself into the social sphere with ancestral relish, joining numerous class elections, secret societies, and regattas. His father, grandfather, and great-grandfather had all been coxswains for the Harvard lightweight crew, and to Loring, the sight of Chamberlin's lean torso skimming over the water, borne forth by the tanned forearms of his fellows, carried with it an aura of perpetuity and rightness.

Loring was not popular at college, where life is a play in which the actors forget any divisions between themselves and the characters they are impersonating. The strikes chalked against him by his peers were legion. He didn't bother concealing his disdain for minstrel shows and clog dances, which were beloved pastimes. It was considered odd that he didn't use tobacco. In a history of Boston literary luminaries, a well-meaning former professor printed the unhelpful suggestion that had Loring "been a bold, swaggering fellow who wore loud trousers and played the banjo, he might have been quite a favorite." In his natural state, the poet was thought far too sensitive and excitable to be a good presiding officer. Indeed, when several campus trees blew over during the

September hurricane of 1869, his hall-mates found his alarm, excitement, and fruitless efforts to help so amusing that the storm was memorialized in the yearbook as "the night Loring battened down the hatches."

Still, his wit won him admirers. The best of his society verse appeared in the *Advocate*, where he was named editor-in-chief, and often asked to read his pieces at class dinners. On the strength of these performances, it was supposed as a matter of course that he would be named class poet, and he had many supporters for the position. But the choice fell instead upon the *nephew* of a distinguished American poet. When questioned about the upset, many among the student body said that they could see no reason for Loring's disfavor; others candidly averred that he was "conceited in the Shakespearean sense," an insult that also acknowledges a certain otherworldly grandeur in the man, perhaps even a flash of the bard.

Loring's revenge was swift and decisive. Two weeks after his defeat, his ballad "The Queen and Elisor" appeared in a magazine called *Old and New*. Replete with "shell-hued cheeks" and "fair knights," "The Queen and Elisor" is not a good poem, but its publication was a credit to Harvard nevertheless, and certainly more than the reigning class poet had achieved. Within a week, Loring and Chamberlin's room was littered with scented envelopes from ladies seeking autographs. Hot on the heels of this triumph, our hero was awarded a $100 cash prize for his senior thesis on the authorship of Shakespeare's tragedies, in which he took the then-controversial stance that they were, in fact, written by Shakespeare.

After this laurel fell at Loring's feet, there was even talk of carrying him in a procession around the Yard. Now no one could doubt his supremacy, save Chamberlin, who worried that such attention might spoil his friend. "If such stuff can do it, I deserve to be spoiled," countered Loring, but the truth is he never really was. If anything, the modest celebrity he enjoyed during the spring of 1870 only cultivated a necessary self-confidence in him, and refined his contempt for base and trivial things. He stayed up late reading Whitman, and became obsessed with opera, especially *Lohengrin*, with its giant swans and crusading knights. In his starriest moments, Loring even talked about quitting Boston for New York City, where he'd charm all the publishers and spend each evening perched in velvet box seats, chatting with the intellectual elite.

But nature was against him, for each spring semester a fog of nostalgia threads through the Harvard elms, transforming the graduating class into misty-eyed confessors. Seniors become freshmen, compelled to pare their initials into desks and weep over their "last" hasty pudding, or "last" Latin exam. Loring was not immune. Consider, for instance, the following anecdote from an early anthology featuring "The Queen and Elisor." Late May, and the two friends were hiking through a hayfield near Lake Quinsigamond, where last summer's bales collapsed like rotting mammoths. Chamberlin, fresh from a European holiday, was describing the plays he'd seen and the people he'd met at parties, when Loring interrupted, saying, "Now, I just want to say here that I have missed you very much, and I hope we shall never be separated so long again." Just then, the earthly remains of a long-dead housecat appeared in the gentlemen's path, orange fur still clinging to its ribcage. "There, look at that," gasped Loring, chapfallen, his arm outstretched to stop his friend. "Nature no longer abhors a vacuum, but I believe she does abhor sentiment!"

***

On the afternoon that this stereogram was taken, Fred W. Loring has been living on the frontier for eight months, but he still feels uneasy in his campaign clothes, like they are a costume or a uniform. He *seems* comfortable leaning against Evil Merodach, but really he is ready to leap clear of the beast at any second, if/when he shifts his weight unexpectedly, or emits his trademark earsplitting bray.

Evil Merodach and Fred W. Loring aren't especially close. The pinned ears are a dead tell, even if the animal's expression remains inscrutable. An aged john used to packing luggage, not poets, Evil Merodach was rented for Loring three weeks prior to this photo session at a trading post in what is now Yavapai County, Arizona. Since then, he has thrown Loring seven times, trampled his hat twice, and relieved himself at several inconvenient moments, including just before this exposure was taken—which may account for Loring's expression.

For these and other injustices, when O'Sullivan asked after the mule's name for the stereogram caption, Loring told him "Evil Merodach." This joke deserves further investigation. A minor character, Evil Merodach is mentioned just twice in the Bible (Jeremiah lii. 31; II Kings xxv. 27), where his uncharacteristically kind treatment of an imprisoned "king of Judah" indirectly leads to the fall of Babylon and his own execution. Maybe Loring saw a version of himself in the Babylonian king's willingness to sacrifice his own life for his forbidden friend. This much is clear: even if Loring didn't intend symbolism, he certainly knew that reading the mule's ridiculous name on the back of the stereogram card would make Chamberlin laugh.

On the warm nights of that last spring term, the two of them used to climb out onto Grays' sleeping porch just as curfew cleared the Yard of war-whooping baseballers, drunk on ale. It was far cooler there than in the dormitory below, and while sprawled across the damp slates they founded a new literary journal to serve as a national stage for Loring's poems and Chamberlin's plays, freeing them from the constraints of editorial prejudice and heathens who didn't want to read quatrains about swans. During one of their last nights on campus, before everything went wrong, Loring outlined how they'd spend afternoons rowing gilt catamarans up and down the Seine, then evenings half-reading manuscripts from hopeful supplicants in libraries gleaming with brushed furs. And maybe it was the weather, or the wine, but in the dark Chamberlin let their lips brush too, just once, like a promise.

Whenever Evil Merodach's saddle pinched his knees, or the frontier heat made him itchy, Fred W. Loring inadvertently conjured up that ghost of a chance. He was annoyed to realize that he was just a beaten dog still wagging at its master's stick. Of course he'd made new friends on the expedition—O'Sullivan was a man he could talk to, and the hired Mojave guides also took an interest, riding alongside Evil Merodach's outside shoulder to shield both poet and mule from the canyon below. But none of these fellow travelers drew close enough for Loring to confide his real reasons for going west, and he didn't discuss the decision with anyone in Boston before he left for Arizona. Therefore, Loring's reasons for leaving were clouded by the agendas of those he left behind, friends who would prefer to pretend he liked girls.

According to Frank Preston Stearns, Loring's friend and biographer, after the runaway success of "The Queen and Elisor," the young writer grew infatuated with a Massachusetts senator's raven-haired daughter. Stearns claims he was seen "dancing about her on the sidewalk on her way from school." Concerned that his darling would meet her ruin in a poet's arms, the senator allegedly paid Loring to quit Boston and forget the girl. In this version of the story, a friend in New York City was the last to speak with our jilted hero. Drunk on strong liquor, he vowed to "make a fame that would win the love of the girl whose love he lived for." This false account convinced some, and indeed, the well-meaning Stearns, who had helped Loring establish a foothold in the Boston press, cannot be blamed for inventing it. He was only giving his protégé what he thought he must—an easy closet to back into, should history need one to permit "The Queen and Elisor's" inclusion in poetry anthologies. Alas, he underestimated Loring's almost pathological need to have the last word.

It is known that on the Class of 1870's graduation night, during a lavish party held at the family home on Massachusetts Avenue, young master Chamberlin announced his betrothal to a peanut-nosed ice heiress he'd been seen in public with only twice before. While the other guests toasted this happy news with good champagne, Loring let himself assume for a dizzy moment that this meant he and Chamberlin would spend their twenties meeting in secret while his oblivious wife devoted herself to his brood, two towheaded babes conceived as further armor against discovery. In an instant, he decided he could come to like children, if they were Chamberlin's, or if they were little girls with curls—he would be their Uncle Fred, and direct them in amateur theatricals.

Of course, these were but the hollow fantasies of a desperate man. At the end of the evening, Chamberlin made it clear that his engagement marked the dissolution of their intimacy by leading a gin-soaked lampoon of "The Queen and Elisor" to the great enjoyment of all assembled, save Loring. When confronted, Chamberlin was distant, saying only that he hoped they'd see each other at class reunions, and wishing him the best with his writing career. Loring reacted badly to Chamberlin's proffered handshake, and the ensuing struggle left one of Boston's leading lights with a broken nose.

This would have been a scandal, had Loring not played drunk as soon as he realized he'd drawn blood. As it was, everyone forgave him at once. Still, pride drove him to quit Boston the day after the party. Perhaps he had already been considering the offer from *Appleton's Journal* to accompany Lieutenant George Montague Wheeler's geographical survey through the Arizona Territory before he boxed Chamberlin; perhaps not. Either way, the journal had offered him an advance of $300.00, plus carte blanche regarding the content and subject of his articles. Coincidentally, this sum was enough to pay for his first novel to be released by his uncle's publishing house while he was encamped on the far side of Death Valley, writing dispatches from the frontier. *In toto*, the plan was well engineered to disguise Loring's wounded flight from Boston as a brilliant new chapter in a promising literary career—and it would have worked beautifully, had the novel in question been anything other than *Two College Friends*.

Part *roman à clef*, part historical fantasy, *Two College Friends* is the maudlin tale of a star Harvard athlete and his reclusive roommate, both from the class of 1864. The youths enlist in the Union Army, where they forge an attachment "passing the love of women." When Ned dies from war wounds, Tom must carry on alone. Crestfallen, Tom marries and conceives a son. At the novel's end, Tom's wife volunteers to name the newborn "Ned," an odd choice that hints at a ghostly godfatherhood while simultaneously signaling her easy acceptance of her husband's one true love.

If the plot and sentiment of *Two College Friends* seems pointed, the first line of the novel's tart preface (penned in the bleak hours between Chamberlin's public betrayal and Loring's abrupt departure from Boston) reveals its author's habitual inability to resist twisting the knife. To whit:

"My dear Friend,

Indignation at my dedicating this book to you will be useless, since I am at present three thousand miles out of your reach. Moreover, this dedication is not intended as a public monument to our friendship; *I know too much for that.*

For Mr. Wm. W. Chamberlin."

***

The bifurcated view. The blur to one from two. Loring himself had so often been that boy kneeling with the stereoscope, dreaming himself into the fairyland that swam before his aching eyes. After a bout of dehydration-induced double vision in Death Valley, seven months into the expedition, he took a keen interest in optics. He tried to watch each time O'Sullivan disappeared behind his buglike tripod, his head and shoulders swallowed by the camera's black cape. Now that they neared the end of the Wheeler Survey, the photographer had started taking posed portraits of his fellow journeymen. A common technique in stereographic series of the mid-19th century, these stills were meant to be viewed after the armchair explorer finished all the buffalo, native caravans, and looming buttes—a kind of primitive credit sequence, a who's who. Seized by enthusiasm for technology, of course Loring leapt at the chance to be shot.

It is essential to recall, as we look at his image, that just a few days before this stereogram was taken, this same man wrote: "I am bootless, coatless, everything but lifeless. I have had a fortnight of horrors. This morning an Indian fight capped the climax. However, I am well and cheerful." It is important to know that in the photograph, Loring's left hand is in his pocket because he has been touching his stagecoach ticket all afternoon, thinking of ivy and bricks and home until the cardboard edges are as frayed as his nerves.

In the morning he is scheduled to ride down the La Paz road to San Bernardino, then north to San Francisco, where he'll catch the Overland Flyer. He is optimistic yet cautious, having decided to use the journey home for metamorphosis. Upon awakening in his berth each morning, he'll shave in the swaying mirror, tuck in a chrysanthemum, and assemble a winning smile. Eastward bound through Chicago, he will alight on the platforms of one-horse towns and practice flirting with the sandwich girls who sell watery egg salad. When he reaches Boston, he'll look up O'Sullivan's cousin, the one the fellows said was pretty when her picture got passed around the fire. He would give it the old college try, and see if Chamberlin might speak to him again now that he, too, had joined life's grand masquerade.

Who knows who Fred W. Loring might have been, had he managed to peel the scales from his eyes, and see his beloved Chamberlin for what he was? He might have had a career in the Boston press, where he was well liked enough to sustain a regular column. Or he could have gone on to New York after all, and fallen in with the crowd at Niblo's, where he would have met a broad-shouldered German juggler who *spreche nur ein bißchen Englisch* but loves to hear poetry read aloud, *sehr musikalische, sehr schön.*

Instead, on the morning of November 5th, 1871, Fred W. Loring was in Arizona trying to hug a mule goodbye. Having never owned a pet, the young poet was confused and surprised by the pain he felt at their separation. During the many hours he spent perched atop Evil Merodach, he'd developed a begrudging trust in the mule's celebrated surefootedness, and come to know the subtle tonal variation between a frustrated snort and a contented one. As he scratched Evil Merodach's rough neck, Loring wondered who, if anyone, would smash the horseflies that landed on him now. Just before leaving, he picked some green tanglehead and served it to the mule in his hat. Evil Merodach's ears stayed pinned to his skull as he ate, but Loring read this as a mark of his friend's constancy, and turned to board the San Bernardino stage with wet eyes.

According to William Kruger, the military clerk who took the seat next to Loring, the ride was crowded but merry, with all the passengers in high spirits, "especially Loring, who anticipated a speedy return to his friends back East." The poet retained his inside seat until the stagecoach rattled into Wickenburg, where they had to change horses due to a lost shoe. "After leaving there, he preferred an outside seat, to which I most decidedly objected," claimed Kruger. "I had two revolvers and he had none, in fact, no arms whatsoever." Loring then laughed off his chivalrous offer of a gun, declaring, "My dear Kruger, we are now comparatively safe. I have traveled with Lieutenant Wheeler for nearly eight months, and have never seen an Indian." After that, Kruger writes, "the first warning I had was the driver's cry: 'Apaches! Apaches!'"

Kruger said that the natives lay concealed behind some rocks, but he recognized them immediately as members of the nearby Deer Creek Reservation, "those so-called 'friendly' Indians whom Uncle Sam feeds and clothes." The riders launched the first volley of bullets, hitting poor Loring, the driver, and another outside passenger. They also shot the off-lead horse. Startled, the rest of the team galloped forward about twenty yards, then drew to a sudden halt, flinging Loring's body headfirst from the stage. At the same moment, the Apaches fired their second volley from three sides, killing all the remaining passengers save Kruger (who clipped two assailants with his revolver) and one Miss Mollie Sheppard, the only woman on the stage, who he dragged unconscious from the bloody scene "by the grace of God alone." "Loring, poor boy, was not mutilated," assures Kruger in the newspaper report, implying that sometime during his heroic escape and rescue he had a quiet moment to assess his slain seatmate's corpse. "He looked calm and peaceful, excepting his fearful wounds to the head."

There are a number of questionable points in Kruger's account. We know that Loring was not naïve about tribal aggression, given his written accounts of his travels with the Wheeler Expedition, so his outright refusal of a revolver seems unlikely, as does the insinuation that he wouldn't know how to use one. The bravado Kruger assigns to Loring also does not match the poet's documented tendency to panic in a crisis.

Furthermore, although the attackers involved in what came to be known as the Wickenburg Massacre did indeed ride from the nearby Date Creek Reservation, they were Yavapai, not Apache, as Kruger claimed. He also purposefully misconstrued the tribe's relationship with area settlers, in a bid to buttress his reputation as a pioneer hero. Months before the Wheeler Survey arrived in Arizona, the people of Wickenburg had promised that the tribe could remain on their ancestral lands, only to force them into a government encampment to the north. The Yavapai plan was simple. They knew mostly uniformed men traveled on the San Bernardino stage, and figured killing a random selection of government officials would send a clear and fair message about what was owed to them.

They didn't know or care that shooting the young man who rode atop the stagecoach would cause his mediocre poetry to appear in numerous anthologies until the turn of the century, after which everything about him was slowly forgotten except a souvenir stereogram that makes him look like a cowboy. And why should they? The Yavapai riders couldn't know that this so-called "massacre" would not advance their cause, that their land would remain under the control of the American government, including the rustic-looking knot of graves now repurposed as an "Indian country" tourist attraction just outside Wickenburg, Arizona.

So Fred W. Loring, cowboy-poet, watched the horses' shadows race as he sailed the San Bernardino stage westward through an ocean of dust. He dared himself to ride outside, speeding shotgun through a Fordian wide shot of red crags and cacti, his left hand knuckled around the threadbare cushion (glued to the seat), his right hand pressing his hat to his head. And of course Loring had the cocky thought *if he could see me now*, because it was a moment of wild abandon unlike any he'd known when they were together—but then he stopped himself, because he was done imagining his life's high points as short plays put on for Chamberlin's benefit.

There were hoofbeats to the north, and our hero glanced at the driver, who mouthed back "buffalo?" just as the first shot whizzed past Loring's right temple. The second connected, flinging his body headfirst from the speeding stage. The poet lay in a twisted heap as the horses galloped away, unable to turn away from his last sight on Earth: a vertical horizon shimmering with visible heat, Arizona cracked into red land and blue sky. Gunshots like popcorn punctuated the hiss in his bloody ears.

Then all at once Fred W. Loring felt pleasantly warm, and the thin oxygen reaching his occipital lobe during this last sip of life allowed him to believe, with utter conviction, that the silhouette he saw resolving along the horizon was not a mirage, but a lonesome mule, broken free to follow him home.

MOTION STUDIES

Plate 1: Horse. (Occident), trackside. (.051 second)

Dawn in Palo Alto, and a brown colt spooks at a white racetrack.

He does not know that his grooms salted the dirt before dawn, sifting the whiteness through coffee cans by moonlight, humming *corridos*. His kind has only two categories for things: familiar and unfamiliar. The brown/white racetrack is both/and. There is no word for uncanny in his language.

The horse looks hard at the twelve black boxes ranged along the fence line, and stares at the beardy stranger stooping to adjust them. The stranger drifts through the black frame of the horse's blinkers, evading close examination. But even from afar, he smells like a barn fire—all burnt hooves and plaster. These un/familiar things make the horse plunge against his traces like a harpooned whale.

Then his man sidles back into frame, murmuring easy son, easy now. The horse likes his man, likes the carrots in his vest pocket, licks his salty palm.

Calms down some.

Plate 2: Man (Stanford) pacing, with ornamental cane.

By 1878, Leland Stanford is the ex-governor of California, with all the rights and privileges appertaining thereto. He also keeps a Standardbred stock farm just outside Palo Alto. Someday this man will found a university. For now he spends his winnings on lavish backstretch parties, magnets for fellow railroad magnates, where he serves abalone and gin and everyone still calls him "the governor." If he's running a favorite, ice sculptures, like promises, are ordered weeks in advance. These are the sorts of parties that would attract movie stars if the movies existed. (Wait for it.)

It is important to remember that it was Stanford's ceremonial sledgehammer that drove the golden spike into the last tie of the Central Pacific railroad, an act that made him symbolically responsible for America's inexorable shift to steam power. Given this history, his obsession with breeding the world's greatest trotter can be read as an apology of sorts. Every dollar and hour he pours into his horses is a private tithe for his part in the species' ongoing obsolescence, for the thousands of unemployed stagecoach and Pony Express mounts that his iron horse daily tramples in its smoky wake. Stanford spends Sundays thumping colts' shoulders in his stock barns, matching Thoroughbred broodmares to champion trotters, engineering speed. He perfects only what is essential: head, hoof, heart.

If pressed, Stanford will reverently outline his belief that every racehorse's gallop contains an infinitesimal moment where he hovers, untrammeled, four feet escaping the ground in perfect defiance of gravity. He reasons that the colts who remain airborne longest must be the fastest, since they needn't waste precious energy propelling themselves aloft. Stanford would be the first to admit that he is no scientist. He can only illustrate his ideas with gestures and oratory. But sometimes, when the light is right in Palo Alto, he swears he's proven his pet theory with the naked eye. We know this because it is what he talks about in bars.

Stanford considers himself above the spit-palm superstition common among horsemen. He places no faith in the backstretch notion that it's bad luck to change an animal's name. In fact, it was he who singled out 'Wonder' two years ago, hoping to re-brand the nondescript brown colt with the indefatigable spirit of the west, a name like a freight train, California-proud:

oc·ci·dent

n.

1. Western lands or regions; the west.

2. The countries of Europe and the Western Hemisphere.

[Middle English, from Old French, from Latin occidens, occident-, from present participle of occidere, *to set (used of the sun), to fall, go down*; see **occasion.**]

Stanford remembers slamming the dictionary shut, triumphant. There was a masculine thud to the word, a finality that felt like a hammer driving steel home. One could speculate that this facility with names and naming was what made Stanford grant Eadweard Muybridge an audience. The Englishman had shown up at the ex-governor's estate unannounced, claiming to be a photographer. For Stanford, reading that first calling card was like receiving a telegram from a wizard. U, unpronounceable! When the man himself followed, sporting an extravagant beard stained with tobacco and halide salts, Stanford had to hear him out.

Muybridge claimed he could answer what he called "the galloping question." He spread his blueprints on the redwood floor like picnic blankets, then knelt beside them to trace axes with his index finger, his enthusiasm smudging the lines. Stanford admired the efficiency of the design, the way it echoed things he already understood. Twelve stereoscopic cameras arranged at regular intervals, like railroad ties, their shutters rigged to trip whenever anything ran past. Photography at forty-four feet per second, said Muybridge. Machines that stop time. He only needed a horse. Horses were better than dogs or cows, because they could be made to run in a straight line.

"I've got just the one," said Stanford, pouring more gin.

Occident was popularly known as "the California Wonder" by 1872. A harness and turf racer noted for his abnormally lengthy stride and domination on the home stretch, he was a favorite among the local press, and the subject of many fine engravings. People bet on the horses they saw in the papers, so Occident's involvement was a shrewd move. Stanford considered himself a man of some poetry. It pleased him to point to the colt as evidence of modern Californian superiority, to put a horse whose very name meant "West" up against the ringers that the East brought by train—*his* train!—and watch him outrun all comers.

But now Stanford paces trackside, frozen mid-stride, fearing imminent fiasco. The sun beats the freshly limned track, bakes his shoulders through his suit. He shades his eyes with a rolled newspaper and winces when the colt shies at the flapping tarpaulin. That's just what he needs, his prize horse making an ass of himself. The newspaper finds its way into his sweating palms, gets wrung like a neck. He regrets placing a large bet on today's outcome, wishes he hadn't invited the small cluster of reporters who lean over the rail, yellow notepads tucked under plaid sleeves.

But he's in charge of the starting gun, so he's got to hold it together.

Plate 3: Man (Muybridge) walking, slight limp in right foot.

By the time the colt is ready, the sun is higher than he'd like.

The photographer knows horses are seldom predictable, despite mankind's claims to control them with leather and metal. The stagecoach crash taught him that. The papers reported that he was caught under the wagon tongue for just a few seconds. But that was long enough to learn how a second can stretch, looping back onto itself. In dreams, black legs churn like pistons above him. He hears the men shouting to pull him out, the horses screaming, all hollow, as if sounding through water. Then hooves like razorblades, shearing his scalp. The shock of exposure. Fade in/out.

Since then, he's only existed at shutter speed.

The doctors called it an orbitofrontal trauma, a bruise to the brain's "emotional center." He was shown the afflicted region on a white ceramic symbolical head, and told to expect consequences, racing thoughts, erratic behavior, et cetera. He took up photography soon after, hoping to recover the vision he had beneath the stagecoach, the fantasy of frozen time. Now he cannot apprehend anything without trapping it in film, pressed like a moth.

The photographer can transfer a fresh exposure to the orange glow of his portable darkroom in less than three seconds without spilling a drop of emulsion, five seconds for the cameras placed farthest away. For weeks, he has conducted private relays in the recesses of his San Francisco studio, perfecting electro-shutters and zoetropes and chronometers, devising names for these devices, skidding past them in his stocking feet.

He prepared for every eventuality, except for the reflective glare generated when California sun hits rock salt. Sudden variables worry him. He has spent months waiting to fracture a second. The trick is choosing the right one. He throws a shy glance at the newspapermen ranged along the rail. He worries about the colt, though it seems calm enough now, pawing at the starting line. He nods at Stanford.

It is time.

Plate 4: Horse galloping. One stride in 24 phases.

From the formula, form the familiar: earth, horse, sky.

You have seen this movie before.

The snick of a projector switch. That dim hummingbird whir.

The horse's right foreleg striking off first, knee drawn up toward open mouth, then thrust forward at an elegant angle; each hoof a wing outstretched.

Back lengthening to compensate, snorting head nodding in time.

The man riding dissolves in under a second, bleached out by sun hitting salt. And there is only the horse, surging.

Flight captured in frames six, thirteen, and twenty-two.

All horses share the common notion that only the rhythmic smack of hooves in near-unison can save the herd from the lion, the coyote, the cowboy's lasso.

It is why every colt's first act on earth is to rise from it, chopstick legs trembling.

The belief that speed can confer immortality is the closest thing they have to a religion.

Horse as *perpetuum mobile*.

It seems no accident then, that Muybridge's horse is Hollywood's first hungry ghost, premiere Sisyphus of the silver screen, mummified in celluloid.

(It was rumored that the camera stole souls.)

The horse runs through the secret half of every movie, the time between frames when we're sitting, oblivious, in the popcorn dark.

He is the blank black space between Orson Welles and Orson Welles and Orson Welles.

If we think of the horse as the key and time as the lock, then everything that happened after Palo Alto was just the door opening.

The discovery that gelatin (obtained by boiling hooves), gum camphor, and gun cotton could produce a faster-developing film, ideal for capturing movement invisible to the human eye.

Muybridge took more photographs, had white grids painted on black walls in a Pennsylvania lecture hall. University funding. The human figure in motion.

Men hammering and jumping and hurling discuses.

Women (nude) mysteriously carrying water pitchers upstairs and down.

Children and lions and wapiti walking. Seven plates devoted to the white-tailed gnu.

But he always came back to the horse. He photographed them leaping, trotting, inexplicably nosing shipping crates past the camera's steady stare.

Each time he shot a horse, Muybridge meticulously wrote out its name, breed, and physical idiosyncrasies. He did not record the people's names.

This says a lot about him.

Hansel	a dark gray Belgian draught horse.
Johnson	a light gray mare, predominantly Percheron.
Hornet	a circus horse, coarse Western grade.
Gazelle	a horse of poor confirmation, straight shoulder, part Standard-bred.
Bob	a horse of poor confirmation, ossification of cartilage in right front foot.
Lotta	an Iceland pony.
Sallie Gardner	chestnut mare, trotter.
Occident	cinema.

OF COURSE,
OF COURSE

Before the Brylcreemed architect and his blonde bride parked their Studebaker Lark in front of the brownstone rancher at 17230 Valley Spring in San Fernando, she'd never heard him mention wanting a pet, let alone one as pricey and demanding as a horse.

It all began on January 5th, 1961, two weeks after the young couple's honeymoon, which we can assume was passionate, based on how often they touch each other in the pilot. The sponsored camera lingers on the Studebaker as the architect scoops his wife over the threshold and kisses her sweaty mouth.

17230 Valley Spring rests on a fashionable cul-de-sac, with a brick patio and Astroturf yard visible from the beige living room's floor-length windows. As a licensed architect (and therefore, an exacting man, a planner), he had the place gutted, then hired a decorator to make sure the appliances (olive green and showroom new) matched the ads every 1961 bride dog-eared in her magazines. As a result, the architect's wife finds her first adult home a lot like church, in that she feels gentle pressure to be awed as she performs the expected rituals, running her manicured fingertips along the olive Formica countertops, swiveling on/off the faucets hot/cold. She beams at her husband, who stands on the patio, arms akimbo, surveying the Dutch-doored garage.

Here, the architect plans to "work from home," an avant-garde notion he developed after suffering nervous exhaustion at his last nine-to-five, where he'd specialized in the design of drive-in hamburger huts. But when he steps into his new home office for the first time, the architect sees that the previous tenant left quite a bit behind, including a ball of barbed wire, some poorly stored rakes, and a gleaming palomino quarter horse.

"Well, how about that—a horse!" cries the architect with boyish joy. It neighs hello.

"Oh, let's get out of here—get him out of here, do SOMETHING!" shrieks the architect's wife, leaping once more into his waiting arms. Overwhelmed by the thought of taking domestic responsibility for a husband *and* a horse (American wifehood then came standard with an unpaid housekeeper position), she goes inside to call the ASPCA. The woman who answers the phone says the shelter has no room for livestock. Instead, she offers the number of a local horse trader who will buy the animal sight unseen for fifty whole dollars, if they aren't interested in keeping it, that is.

When the architect's wife returns to tell her husband the good news, he is already grooming the horse with a brush he found. It just doesn't feel right, he muses, to put it out of house and home, even if its home is now theirs. Having never read *Black Beauty*, the architect's wife reassures him that horses don't mind being sold; they probably enjoy getting to see different parts of the country, meet new people, and try new things. To her credit, she does not mention dog food or glue factories, even when the horse trader pulls up with his ramshackle flatbed. The horse limps when money is exchanged, and only recovers after the trader drives off-screen, calling them a couple of crooks.

"See, honey? He wants to stay," says the architect, patting the horse's neck, finding it not at all odd that everything worked out just so.

The architect's wife admits it is a pretty horse, with well-fed flanks that glint like fresh pennies in the late afternoon sun. But the animal's health and beauty also arouse her suspicion. She's sure something so large and expensive and alive would never simply be forgotten, even in the most chaotic of moves.

"There must be a good reason why it was left behind," she thinks aloud.

The architect quips about gift horses and mouths.

The new horse marred the candlelit occasion of the couple's first dinner in their new home by smudging its rubbery muzzle repeatedly against the dining room's plate glass window, then baring grass-stained teeth at the underdone pot roast. A city girl, her creature encounters restricted to picture books, zoos, and an aunt's elderly terrier, the architect's wife had thought animals weren't smart enough to realize that their faces and our faces are the same thing. But the truth was they always look you right in the eye, even as they bite or scratch or kick. The circus camel she'd been forced to ride when she was ten taught her that much, Maybelline lashes blinking as it deposited a warm gob of clover drool atop her sweet pigtailed head.

Ignoring his wife's obvious misgivings, the architect designs his new office around the existing box stall, favoring a Western motif. Despite investing in tack and cowboy boots, he seldom rides his horse. Instead, he prefers to whimsically incorporate it into their daily life, as a child would a favorite stuffed animal. For instance, he takes it along on their zoo date so it can "meet the zebras," and purchases a small television set for the barn so it won't "get bored" when left to its own devices.

A city girl, the architect's wife doesn't know enough about horses to judge whether it is odd for them to escape as often as this one does, or be so destructive. One afternoon it crushes a new patio chaise, luxuriously stretching its hooves through the striped rubber webbing. Another, it noses through the neighbor's mail, leaving an unpaid parking ticket shredded under the silk chrysanthemums. There are several neighborhood incidents involving laundry and manure.

It is, in short, the worst horse. Still, the architect says the scent of hay and warm leather stirs something deep and lost within him, a wildness he hasn't felt since boyhood trail overnights at Camp Nawakwa. It speaks to him, he tells her, pinball eyes manic.

"That's nice, dear," replies the architect's wife.

At night she lies awake in her MPAA-sanctioned twin bed, wishing he'd creep into hers, as he did on their honeymoon. Before they wed, the architect had promised her a life of ease and adventure. Now he won't leave his horse alone overnight. Which isn't to say he never tries; for their second anniversary, to his credit, he books the penthouse suite at the Chateau Marmont, but they end up having to cancel when the horse colics on a pineapple Jell-O mold Mrs. Addison left on her windowsill.

"I'll make it up to you next year, dear," says the architect.

"It's okay," lies the architect's wife, pushing her electric mixer against the bowl so hard the beaters clatter on the Pyrex.

***

After three seasons spent in her gleaming kitchen, creaming yolks and chopping scallions for the deviled eggs her husband left half-eaten on his drafting table, the architect's wife finds a hobby of her own. She enrolls in a night course at the local art college, where she also disrobes thrice weekly so bearded beatniks and sweater-clad co-eds might draw and sculpt her curvaceous form. She likes to imagine her nude blondeness perched on easels throughout the Valley, all those hungry eyes on her or simulacra of her—the thought makes her feel desired in a way her husband can't or won't, now that he believes himself to be the chosen mouthpiece of a sentient equine. After each class, she lets the patchouli-scented teacher's assistant press her thighs into the quilted upholstery of the architect's once-prized Studebaker Lark, then drives home to perfume herself back into his adoring wife.

She becomes adept at keeping up appearances, at ushering the architect into hallways when he brings up his horse at cocktail parties, her smile discreet, her skirt swaying like a bell. Her macramé owls are sold at all the church bazaars, and she spearheads a bake sale to fund-raise for the local youth center. Come summer she tans on the patio, the scalloped elastic of a purple department store bikini cutting into her childless hips as she watches the horse browse among her begonias.

When her husband emerges from the barn to retrieve his pet, she feigns sleep behind tortoiseshell sunglasses. She's found that, like an alcoholic, he is at his most tractable when allowed to think he's successfully camouflaged his problem. Chief among his delusions is the idea that his wife cares deeply about the lawn, which remains an Astroturf dream even though it never rains in this iteration of San Fernando. He yanks his horse's mouth away from the flowerbed and joins in with the canned laughter, thinking he's evaded her wrath.

Theirs is a sexless marriage. By their sixth anniversary, between starting a backyard juice bar, helping the actress Zsa Zsa Gabor overcome her fear of riding, and his sudden delusion that he and his horse are now agents for something called the Secret Intelligence Agency, the architect has grown worn and thin. When his wife expresses frustration that he hasn't ever wanted to start a family, he martyrs himself by sleeping in the barn. It isn't funny anymore. At the supermarket, the neighbor ladies corner the architect's wife between the glossy fruit pyramids, asking when they'll hear the pitter-patter of little feet. Blithe with amphetamines, she sighs, "Oh, we're trying," then steers her cart toward the carrots, piled high and damp with refrigerated mist.

That night, the architect claims his horse won a color T.V. in a radio giveaway and explains that he has installed it in the barn instead of the living room, since that's only fair. But his wife still doesn't leave. She has come to relish the unbridled freedom her husband's psychosis provides. While he wastes afternoons in the barn, making crank calls in an odd cowboy drawl, she cruises the Valley high on Obetrol, the Beach Boys, and not doing the laundry—a real California girl.

A competent draughtsman, she works on her husband's blueprints while he snores away in his bed, so he won't embarrass himself in front of clients. It should upset her how easily the architect leapt to the conclusion that his horse finishes them—an equine Frank Lloyd Wright—but his delusions have become commonplace. She listens when he announces how *glad* he is to get this project done so *fast*, how the idea for the fountain in the central atrium hit him like a bolt out of the blue, boy, that horse must be some kind of lucky charm. The architect's wife beams politically, says she's so glad he's doing so well.

Of course of course she knows it's impossible, the exhausted delusion of an overtired mind, the unavoidable side effect of her double life. But one day, while the architect's wife is hanging laundry, the horse noses open its Dutch door with sitcom aplomb, winking those Maybelline eyes. And she knows, with sudden sharpness, that someday still more will be asked of her. If she stays, she will need to pay somehow for her unlikely deliverance from Tupperware parties and bridge nights.

The architect's wife wonders, not for the first time, what happened to the previous inhabitants of 17230 Valley Spring in San Fernando, the couple—she's sure it was a couple—who left their golden horse behind. Swept up in the aftermath of her new husband's joy at keeping the gelding, she'd never asked the neighbors whose it really was, what kind of people abandon a horse. Still, she knows in her bones that when the former homeowners drove away, it wasn't like they forgot to grab the dish rack, or left some paint in the garage sink that matched the baseboards. Leaving the horse here had been a ridding, a casting out.

The architect's wife feels unsafe. In her nightmares, blonde babies wearing her face slide off the horse's broad yellow back and fall through the patio like it's a pool.

***

In the final episode of the sixth and last season of their marriage, the A-plot follows the architect as he tries to stop his horse from pursuing a career in veterinary medicine. The B-plot deals with the architect's wife's aged father injuring himself while trying to help her with household chores. Each time the old man gets hurt, his misfortune is either directly or indirectly blamed on the architect, who is, as usual, preoccupied with his horse's shenanigans.

Meanwhile, the architect's wife is made to do uncomfortable things, such as rubbing Ben-Gay into her groaning dad's hairy back. He strained it moving furniture that her husband (it is heavily implied) should have been there to move. During this awkward family tableau, the architect, sporting a horrible cardigan, arrives to announce that he's just returned from chasing his horse through the college campus. The architect's wife asks her spouse how on Earth the horse made it all the way to campus, and he replies (his earnestness total) that maybe it found a student bus ticket!

Still new enough here to be shocked, the old man twists around on the chaise lounge. His face is a rictus of disappointment in his daughter's sexual choices. His greasy back glistens like lunchmeat in the high key light.

The architect's wife tells her husband to finish his father-in-law's back massage, tosses the bottle of liniment at him, and walks off-screen.

***

That night, she sits awake in her twin bed, so much like the one she grew up in, wringing her fingers and wondering how her life came to this. The glare of her bedside lamp stirs the architect, who rolls over to grab and read his alarm clock.

"It's two o'clock, what are you doing up so late?"

"Thinking," she tells him.

"About what?"

"About the kook I married."

Laughter. The architect scrambles to his wife's side, but she stiffens at his touch. She asks "Why do you hate my father so much?" but she's really asking, for the last time, why she should remain married to someone who's much more interested in his trick pony than the woman who's stood between him and the loony bin for years.

Oblivious, the architect keeps telling his wife that if she doesn't want him around, she should just say so, and he'll go sleep in the barn. He repeats this line several times, and each time he sounds more like a teenage boy begging to get grounded in his room with his comic books and records. It is unclear, as ever, how him sleeping elsewhere would affect her, given their separate beds. He does not make it sound like a punishment, then slinks downstairs with his pillow, visibly wounded, when she agrees he should go.

This is the last scene that ever features the architect's wife.

It is easy to leave her where the camera does, alone in a dowdy nightgown, staring at the closet where she keeps her luggage, obviously making a choice. It is easy to forget about her because the camera hasn't ever acknowledged her as anything more than a live-in housekeeper, a nosy threat or hindrance to the architect's harmless fun. The episode's rollicking conclusion centers on the architect assisting with triage in his horse's new backyard veterinary clinic, which is already all the rage among the animal set. The woman of the house isn't mentioned again, not even when her dad slips off the box he's using to spy on his son-in-law, and konks himself unconscious. The architect manages to convince the old man that the baby elephant, goat, and Holstein cow he saw in the barn were hallucinations. As he helps the injured man up, the architect does not worry aloud whether his wife heard any of this brouhaha.

But every second he doesn't acknowledge her continuing existence could also mean she's gotten away clean. As the credits roll, the architect's wife is speeding away in her Studebaker Lark, olive green scarf whipping around blonde hair and tortoiseshell sunglasses, disco on the wind. She is remembering that her given name is Carol, not sweetie or honey or the architect's wife. And when her mouth tries out the sound, it's like a spell that lets her remember there are other places in this automatic nation, whole modern cities with apartments and offices and freeways, where people never see horses except on T.V.

PRIOR APPEARANCES

"Motion Studies" appeared in *The Portland Review*. "Shooting A Mule" appeared in *Redivider*, and was anthologized in *Among Animals Two*, from Ashland Creek Press. "The Mammoth Horse Waits" appeared in *cream city review*. "Shooting A Mule" appeared in *Redivider* and *Among Animals Two*, from Ashland Creek Press. "Two On A Horse" appeared in *The Indiana Review* and *Guesthouse*. "One Trick Pony" appeared in *Big Muddy: A Journal of the Mississippi River Valley*, and was anthologized in *Among Animals Three*, from Ashland Creek Press. "Granddad Swam" appeared in *Oyez Review*. "Of Course, Of Course" appeared in *Animal: A Beast of A Literary Magazine*. "Midwest Utilitor Breakdown" appeared in *The Poydras Review*. "The Lost Hoof of Fire Horse #12" appeared in *Footnote: A Literary Journal of History*. "Lady, The Mind-Reading Mare" appeared in *The Cossack Review* and *The SFWP Quarterly*. "Based On A True Story" appeared in *StoryQuarterly*. "Fred W. Loring and His Mule, 'Evil Merodach,' 48 Hours Before Death" appeared in *Laurel Review* and *The Winter Anthology*. "Stock Footage" appeared in *Chariton Review*.

ACKNOWLEDGMENTS

Thank you to my partner, Michael Matthews. The small key is lost!

Thank you to my mother, Julie Bowers, my dad, Greg Bowers, and my brother, Mike Bowers.

Eternal gratitude to Karen Grindler and the whole herd at Cedar Creek Therapeutic Riding Center for more adventures, laughter, food, and love than I can ever hope to repay. This place changes lives: https://cedarcreek.missouri.org/

Thank you to a cavalcade of teachers, writers, and dear friends for their support, camaraderie, encouragement, inspiration, and kindness over the years:

Marc McKee, Joanna Luloff, Will Buck, Sharon Emmerichs, Luke Rolfes, Ron Austin, James Brubaker, Chris Iseli, Kevin Hoffman, Angela Colter, Debra Rubino, Bret McCabe, Benn Ray, Rachel Whang, A.A. Balaskovits, Kelly and John Marksbury, Sarah Pinsker, Laura Bogart, Julie and Damon Hawk, Elyse Pineau, Pam Endres, Sarah Smith, Kevin Mayer, Anne and Jack Wagner, Nancy Springer, Catherine Czaya, Christian Sturgis, Nairobi Collins, Beau Finley, Justin Blemly, Bethany and Todd Jones, Andrea Valencia, Nicole Baer, Kyle Anderson, Rob Reichhelm, Sadaya McDonough, Jane Thayer, Rudi Waldschuetz, Adam and Allison Fastman, Jordan Hoffman, Ben Wolman, Lindsey Cornelius, Jenn Blair, Camellia Cosgray, Jen Ayres, Elise Vandover, Benedikte Aarsland, Kristin Bales, Jennifer and Dan Murphy, Carrie Brinser, Anna Conner, Alyson K. Spurgas, Trish Causey, Katharine Zimolzak, Kat Hudson, Marjorie McAtee, Kate Bulinski, Jerad Lewis, Katy Didden, Gabriel Bump, John Paul Spanogle, Scott Cairns, Marcia

Vanderlip, LaTanya McQueen, Emily C. Friedman, Johannes Wich-Schwarz, Dana Levin, Bebe Nickolai, Jesse Kavadlo, Art Santirojprapai, Germaine Murray, Alex Wulff, John Marino, Vaughn Anderson, Kent Bausman, Alden Craddock, Amanda Garrison, John Doerflinger, James Cagle, Lokke Heiss, Deborah Meyerson, Brian and Emily Carter, Madison Smartt Bell, Elizabeth Spires, Mary V. Marchand, R.H.W. Dillard, Pinckney Benedict, Nancy M. West, Marly Swick, Justin and Elaine Arft, the extended Bowers, Hertz, Matthews, and Hill families, and everyone else I'm forgetting to mention.

Thank you to my colleagues and students at Maryville University and the University of Missouri.

Gratitude to Andrew Gifford, Adam Sirgany, Monica Prince, Deesha Philyaw, and the rest of the staff at SFWP for leading this wobbly little foal of a book out into the sunlight.

Thank you to Bama and Roland, for being the best cats a writer could ever ask for.

Thank you to Billy and Teddy, my horses, for being my other childhood dream come true.

And finally, thank you for reading.

ABOUT THE AUTHOR

Jess Bowers lives in St. Louis, Missouri, where she works as an Associate Professor of English and Humanities at Maryville University. Her short stories have won the Winter Anthology Prize and *Laurel Review*'s Midwest Short Fiction Contest. When not writing or reading, she can be found riding horses, exploring museums, and watching too much television. Find her at jessbowers.org.